The Bees and Other Wild Things

Chase Connor

Book Cover Designed by: Allen T. St. Clair, ©2022 Chase Connor & The Lion Fish Press

CHASE CONNOR BOOKS are published by

The Lion Fish Press
539 W. Commerce St #227
Dallas, TX 75208

www.chaseconnor.com
www.thelionfishpress.com

AUTHORS' NOTE:
This is a work of fiction. Names, characters, places, and incidents either are the product of the authors' imagination or are used fictitiously, and any resemblance to actual persons, living or dead, business establishments, events, or locales is entirely coincidental. None of this is real. This is all fiction.

eBook 978-1-951860-43-1
Paperback 978-1-951860-44-8

Also by Chase Connor

LGBTQ+ YA Books

Just a Dumb Surfer Dude: A Gay Coming-of-Age Tale
Just a Dumb Surfer Dude 2: For the Love of Logan
Just a Dumb Surfer Dude 3: Summer Hearts
A Surplus of Light
GINJUH
When Words Grow Fangs
Sending Love Letters to Animals and Other Totally Normal Human Behaviors

LGBTQ+ New Adult/Lit Fic/MM Romance

A Tremendous Amount of Normal
The Gravity of Nothing
Between Enzo & the Universe
The Warmth of Our Closest Star
A Straight Line (w/ co-author J.D. Wade)

LGBTQ+ Magical Realism

Possibly Texas

A Point Worth LGBTQ Paranormal Romances

Jacob Michaels Is Tired (Book 1)
Jacob Michaels Is Not Crazy (Book 2)
Jacob Michaels Is Not Jacob Michaels (Book 3)
Jacob Michaels Is Not Here (Book 4)
Jacob Michaels Is Trouble (Book 5)
CARNAVAL (A Point Worth LGBTQ Paranormal Romance Story)
Jacob Michaels Is Dead (Book 6)
Jacob Michaels Is... The Omnibus Edition (all 6 JMI books and CARNAVAL)
Murder at the Red Rooster Tavern (Book 7)

Erotica

Bully
Briefly Buddies
Jake (A Novella from Tricked: The Men of Briefly Buddies)

Audiobooks

A Surplus of Light: A Gay Coming-of-Age Tale (narrated by Brian Lore Evans)
Between Enzo & the Universe (narrated by Brian Lore Evans; Tantor Media)

Translated

Between Enzo & the Universe – **Spanish**
A Surplus of Light – **Spanish**

Anthologies Contribution

Magis and Maniacs: And Other Christmas Stories (Frank, A Christmas in Pajamas, A Surfer's Christmas, and *The IT Guy)*

Kindle Vella

Tricked: The Men of Briefly Buddies (serialized/episodic continuation of *Briefly Buddies*)

To all the wild things that need no name.

Contents

The crash that was heard through town that fateful night tore people from their sleep, though no one bothered to rise from their beds. Some, when asked later, said the sound was loud enough to wake the dead, though the dead didn't rise to investigate, either. However, as the dead stayed in place, so did the town's residents roll over and slip back into slumber. Flickering taillights and headlights flashed on the main street, the only two stop signs in town looking on from opposite corners.

To this day, only one person knows exactly how long the three victims of the crash remained trapped in their cars as the town slept. A boy, leaning against the side of the convenience store downtown, hiding from his father, heard the ear-splitting crash like the rest of the town. Unlike the rest of the citizens, he had seen the wreck.

The sedan had rolled to a stop at the sign, though at such a late hour, it seemed ridiculous the driver had heeded its demands. No cops were around to issue tickets. No one was around to report the driver in the morning. However, the driver had taken the stop as an opportunity to reach into the passenger seat for her purse. Seconds later, with a squeal of tires, the pick-up truck, coming from the other direction, chose to ignore its sign.

Traveling at a speed more suited for the highway as opposed to the main street in a rural town in Texas, the sound of the pick-up hitting the sedan head-on was a thunderous clap of metal crumpling against metal. Later, though he only ever told one soul, the boy would say that he saw the wreck before he heard it. As though watching a movie at double speed, which was suddenly thrown into slow-motion as the cars collided, the sound seemed to arrive several seconds after the collision.

Maybe it was the shock of seeing the wreck. Or maybe that's how sound works when destiny arrives. The boy saw the wreck before he heard it, even though he was staring at the sedan when the pick-up truck plowed into it. As long as it took for the sound to reach the boy's ears, it seemed to take even longer for the two vehicles to settle after the wreck, and the smoke to begin rising from their decimated front ends.

Stumbling away from the side of the convenience store towards the wreckage, the boy stared with terrified recognition. Due to the shock, he'd never be able to estimate how long he stared in horror, but eventually, the boy ran for help.

Minutes later, with distant sirens carrying on the warm summer night breeze, an anguished howl—that everyone would later describe as belonging to a wounded animal—cut through the air.

And a woman's body was pulled from the sedan as the anguished screaming continued.

Some people in town say you can still hear that scream on warm, silent summer nights.

It was one of the first ways the town became haunted by tragedy.

Chapter 1
CARSON

As far back as recorded history went, the creek had never been so dry. Collective memory, nebulous as it was, told a similar tale. Everyone agreed that each year, around late August, the creek would often get a bit low. Memory served to produce that fact, which everyone seemed to agree upon. However, that year, as May surrendered to June, and after a dearth of rain in spring, the creek went dry. The early summer sun claimed its victim swiftly and mercilessly—practically overnight.

The kids were leaving school for summer one day, and the next morning the creek was gone.

Instead of a ribbon of gently moving, crystal-clear, cool water, a dusty gulch slashed a wound through the woods at the edge of town. The creek wasn't the only victim that summer slaughtered. With no source of water, the sounds of scurrying animals in the underbrush disappeared overnight. The birds no longer sang their odes aloft in the tree branches. Even the trees stopped whispering among themselves, preserving their energy. Just in case. In case of what, I didn't know. The rain wasn't going to return for a long time. Maybe that was the reason for the trees' preparation.

That's what the news had said—that the rain was gone for a while.

I'd heard the old-timers at the coffee shop telling the grade school kids that the creek "just up and walked away in the middle of the night." But "it'll come back soon enough."

That explanation would have made me smile. But I hadn't felt like smiling for a long time. Maybe since the creek had last gone dry.

The old-timers loved to sit around the coffee shop from the time the sun came up until the lunch rush arrived. Then they'd move to the convenience store and gather around the stack of old crates by the side of the building and shoot the shit until the shit was dead, buried, and eulogized. I'd hear them talking about the creek when I'd find time to go into town for groceries. Sometimes, if we didn't need anything from the store, but I had the time, I'd still walk into town. Simply to exercise my legs.

My legs are our most valuable asset. That and my hands.

Speculation from the old men would vary greatly and get wilder as the days dragged by that summer. Theories, from the ridiculous—space aliens and clandestine government operations—to the possible—tapping of water tables by the utility companies and global warming—gave the men something to debate. The fact remained that we hadn't had rain in three months, and a mild winter preceded spring. Theories were unnecessary.

I didn't debate the old men. Anyone younger than Methuselah was automatically dismissed as "not knowin' shit from Shinola" anyway.

These were the same men who whispered, but not quietly enough, about "that Black fella runnin' the Save-A-Ton." Being younger than them, I was fascinated with the way one of the old-timers would simply mention "that Black fella" and they'd all grow silent before nodding knowingly at each other.

It wasn't that I didn't understand the implication of that small phrase, but I wondered how they all knew they agreed. They never said more than that before nodding, so maybe some of them were actually nodding their approval of the "Black fella's" ownership of the store?

They probably didn't think about that. Or maybe they had discussed that phrase's implications thoroughly in the other meetings they had in private at Joe Watson's house on Friday evenings. He was the unofficial leader of the old-timers in town. No one got invited to those meetings, and no one was supposed to know about those meetings, but everyone knew what happened at those meetings.

That "Black fella" was Wallace Lee, the newest owner of the grocery store. Back before I started high school when Ellis and Marilyn Walker got too old to run the Sav-A-Ton—the only grocery store in town—and their kids declined to take it over, they had no choice but to sell. I never repeated it to anyone, but one morning, while doing our grocery shopping, I'd heard Ellis whisper to Marilyn that he didn't want to sell to Wallace Lee. Then they both nodded. I don't know if they agreed with each other.

No one else wanted to buy and operate a grocery store in Podunk, Texas, so Ellis and Marilyn finally had to stop whispering and nodding. In the end, they'd whispered and nodded for a year, the last three months of which Marilyn had been on dialysis. Nine months of no other offers, and three months of suffering on Marilyn's part, and they still turned the store over to Wallace Lee with whispers and nods. It was no sweat off of Wallace's back. He got the Save-A-Ton for a steal once it was apparent that he was the only interested party.

Smalltown America often grows the putrid feed that poisons its own livestock.

Save-A-Ton got better almost immediately under the watchful eyes and patient hands of Wallace Lee. The prices were better, the stock was fresher, he always had more than one cashier on hand, and he started to carry more off-brand items. People gradually stopped listening to the old-timers' and Ellis's and Marilyn's whispers. They stopped paying attention to their nods.

It was never mentioned that maybe they shouldn't have been listening and nodding in the first place.

No apologies were made.

But the new way of doing things saved people money and produced better groceries, so everyone agreed to forgive and forget.

I'm certain Wallace Lee didn't agree.

The white people felt better, so that was all that mattered.

Sometimes Wallace would let me sweep and mop at the end of the day for a bag of groceries. When I had an evening free to do it. Dad's disability checks didn't go far, so the extra help was appreciated, even if it made the groceries taste like acid bitterly boiling up from my stomach. Uncertain about why that was since I had worked for the groceries, I did my best to ignore the feeling.

It wasn't about Wallace Lee.

Nothing bad in our town had anything to do with Wallace Lee's existence.

He was a nice man. And a target for old-timers who never should have been given the time of day.

I stayed away from most of the town gossip anyway.

Staying away from the creek was harder.

Even on a typical summer day, when Texas wasn't experiencing catastrophic droughts, and the creek was full for the local kids' swimming desires, it was peaceful. Something about the laughter and unbridled, exuberant chaos made me think of simpler times. Before high school. When summer was a season to be a kid. Not simply a hotter three months in my life that had become repetitious. A season where I could explore the woods like all of the other kids. Take a leisurely walk whenever I wanted, as I was doing when I nodded to the group of old-timers stationed at their usual spot outside of the convenience store.

Nodding jovially at me as I walked by, the plastic bag dangling from my fingers at my side, the men always greeted me warmly. They'd whisper and nod to each other once my back was to them, that I knew for certain, but it wasn't my concern. The people in town whispered and nodded about everyone. Some of us simply happened to be the target more often than others.

I knew what the men whispered, but I didn't care. Coming into town had served two purposes, and the men's opinions of me wasn't one of them. So, I let my back shield me from their whispers as I made my way down the main street of town, the asphalt so hot it felt as though the well-worn black rubber soles of my shoes were sticking to it. Each step felt as though I was peeling my foot away from the ground.

As I made my way to the edge of town, a gentle breeze ruffled my hair but did nothing to dull the oppressive heat. It was only early July and we'd had triple-digit temperatures for a solid week. Without any rain to alleviate some of summer's symptoms, the days felt like cracked leather that might split at the slightest tug. Nighttime was stuffy, breezeless, and dark. The night closed in around us like a zipper being pulled, trapping the town inside a bag until the sun rose again.

Closer to the woods, the trees blocked the breeze, making the day nearly unbearable, but I continued on the path I'd walked thousands of times before. Inside the tree line, the town shrinking in the distance behind me, I could barely breathe. The stagnant, musty air would have made it feel as though I was trying to breathe underwater if the air hadn't been so dry. So, I suppose it was more like trying to breathe in a dry sauna.

Leaves crackled underfoot but they were not the fallen leaves of the woods going to sleep for autumn. The leaves hadn't heaved their last breath and tossed themselves to the ground after a life well-lived. These were the crackling of leaves assassinated by a cruel summer sun declaring its power over everything upon which it shone.

Typically, even before you get close to the creek, you can hear all of the kids' voices off in the distance, growing louder as you draw nearer. I didn't hear anything. No kids screaming and laughing. No splashes of bodies plunging into the crisp, refreshing water of the creek. No taunts or jokes or indication that any kids had bothered even venturing out to the creek for the day. There were no scurrying critters in the underbrush nearby. The woods were dying. At best, hibernating, waiting for the sky to cloud over and offer relief.

I'd walked this path to the woods so many times, and knew every step to avoid stumbling, that I found myself standing on the cracked and dried bank of the creek within a few minutes. Staring down at the dusty gulch a few yards below should have been depressing, but I couldn't bring myself to feel anything. The hay-like grass on the bank, the skeletal trees, and the brown slash winding its way through the woods felt like an old Spaghetti Western. Brown and gray and, somehow, mournful.

And silent. Even the gentle breeze that the empty creek allowed to blow through the center of the woods, had nothing to say. I'd never seen the woods so barren. So lifeless. So sad. Which was why the sound of crackling on the other side of the creek, a few yards away, made my eyes snap up from staring down at the gulch.

When he stepped out of the trees on the other side of the creek, he didn't notice me at first. I'd arrived before him, so he hadn't had my footsteps to alert him to my presence. Like me, it was clear from the movement of his eyes, that he had come to check out the health of the creek. From his expression, I could tell he was as disappointed as I. I'm not sure how long we stood there on opposite sides of the creek before he noticed me.

When he caught sight of me out of the corner of his eye, and his head snapped up in surprise, a smile slowly appeared on his face. We stared at each other for a moment before he slowly raised his hand. A wordless greeting.

Not really a wave, but a greeting nonetheless.

A moment longer I stared back at him, expressionless.

Then I turned on my heels and headed back out of the woods. I'd seen what I'd come to see, so I let his silent disappointment follow me as I made my way back into town. I don't know why I didn't at least raise a hand in greeting back. Nothing else was required of me. A greeting can be a greeting with no other commitment attached. Ignoring him had been my default for months. That's why I didn't raise my hand. My pride. That was another reason—probably the biggest.

Through the woods, I wound my way along dirt paths, around brambles, and to the far outskirts of town where the woods met its border. Within the cluster of trees at the end of the dirt road that led out to the main road into the town proper, I was back home. Not much more than a shack after decades of neglect, it wasn't much, but it sporadically kept the rain off our heads.

Dad was in his chair on the old wood porch, a blanket draped over his legs to fight off the complete lack of chill in the air. His head had rolled to the side and away from the headrest so that his neck was bent and he was looking up at the weathered wood that comprised the ceiling of the porch. Huffing, I jogged across the drought-cracked dirt yard that was patchy with yellowing weeds and up the stairs to his side.

Setting the bag next to the wheel of his chair, I squatted and gently slid my hands around the back of his head. A soft grunt escaped Dad's throat as I pulled his head forward and repositioned it against the headrest. His eyes stared through me, vacant of recognition or expression. Smiling, I laid my hands on his shoulders.

"That's better, right?" I asked.

As always, he didn't respond. He stared at me as though I wasn't there.

You have to watch Dad when he's resting in his chair. Sometimes his head will roll away from the headrest. If his head simply tips to the side, it's not as big of a deal, since if he drools you can simply wipe it up. When his head tilts back, saliva can pool at the back of his mouth and he can start choking. Unsure of how long his head had been tilted back, I did my best to check his mouth as noninvasively as possible.

He seemed fine, so I checked his bags that hung from his chair. One for each type of bodily waste. Neither needed to be changed yet. He was good to go. I felt his exposed skin and his forehead, the back of his neck. He wasn't overheated. Next, I checked the I.V. bag that hung from the pole that stuck up from the back of his chair.

Dad was good to go on hydration.

His feet hadn't slipped off of the footrests of the chair.

Other than his head tilting back, he was fine.

Dad isn't completely unaware of what's going on around him, and he's not entirely immobile. His movements are incredibly limited and rare due to his disability, however. Feeding and hydrating him orally are practically impossible anymore. It's all tubes and hoses and needles. A sudden muscle spasm can reposition him in his chair, sometimes in a dangerous way. Other times, Dad finds some will deep within him and manages to move a bit, though it's never much. That too can lead to a problem. Unless he's sleeping, Dad needs someone to watch over him.

"He's been out here since you left."

I didn't react to my aunt's voice, but I rose at the sound. My eyes stayed on Dad a moment longer before I raised my eyes to greet her.

"He seems perfectly happy out here in the shade and warmth," she said, crossing her arms over her chest lazily. "At least he's got something pretty to look at while he's hangin' out."

There was no point in telling my aunt that the dirt yard, scarred with crevices from the month-long drought and hot summer sun, along with the ragged weeds, wasn't pretty. I gave her a nod and did my best to fix a smile on my face.

"We've just been doin' our thang," she said. "He's fine."

"Yeah," I said. "He seems fine."

"You get the macaroni?" she asked.

She glanced down at the bag next to my feet. In response, I passed the bag to her. Gleefully, she took the plastic bag with "Sav-A-Ton" in big, bold red letters on its side, and glanced inside. Kraft Macaroni and Cheese. Typically, I'd buy the generic version when I went shopping, but since my aunt was around and she liked "the good stuff," and she was paying, I got the brand name.

I ate a lot of generic mac and cheese because it was cheap. My aunt ate a lot of it because she grew up southern white trash. When she got older, she was still southern, but she made enough money to pretend she wasn't white trash. Except when it came to macaroni and cheese.

"With them pork chops I brought with me, them greens, that can of biscuits, and this," she stared longingly into the bag, "we'll be eatin' good, boys."

Boys. I was twenty-four years old and dad was pushing fifty.

My aunt looked down at my dad, her brother, and laid a pitying hand on his shoulder. I wanted to slap it away.

"Well," she said a little too dramatically for my taste, "two of us will. Won't we?"

Then she looked up at me brightly. I gave her the same smile I'd been giving her since I was fourteen.

"Yup."

She brightened even more. With a squeeze of Dad's shoulder from that pitying hand and a jiggling of the bag at her side, she set her face firmly.

"I'm gonna get started on dinner," she said. "Should be ready in an hour-so."

"Okay."

She started to turn to go back inside but fixed her gaze on me instead.

"You know," she started slowly, "I been thinkin'."

"There's your first problem," I teased.

I wasn't really teasing.

She chuckled. "Now that I done retired from teachin', and Mr. Barton's still got a couple years left at his law firm, I ain't got much to do with my time."

Mr. Barton.

My aunt's name is Sara Lee Barton. No shit. I'm not kidding. She calls her husband "Mr. Barton," probably to make him sound as important as she's made him out to be in her head.

"You gonna sub?" I asked.

"Well, I was thinking maybe you and Jimmy could use me around more often," she said. "Whatcha think-a that? Give you more time to do the things you need to do. Get out more. That sound good?"

Bile threatened to seep up my throat and scald the inside of my mouth. I choked it back.

"That would be appreciated," I said. "If it's not too much trouble."

I didn't want my aunt around. I didn't want anyone around. Because no one had been around for the last decade when they had been needed the most. *Fuck 'em all.*

Sara Lee practically squealed with delight. She reached out and slapped my shoulder happily, then leaned down and kissed the top of Dad's head with a noisy flourish, then dashed inside, the bag of mac and cheese swinging wildly at her side.

Dad grunted.

I reached out and patted down the wisps of his hair her kiss had rustled out of place.

"I feel the same way, Dad," I said.

Certainly, I had no way to know what Dad's grunt meant. But I had a pretty good idea. With a sigh, I sunk into the rickety rocking chair at Dad's side and stared out at the dried yard and the hazy heat it seemed to radiate back up at the sun.

The view wasn't pretty.

Reaching over, I laid my hand upon Dad's that was resting on the arm of his chair and gave it a squeeze. He grunted again.

"Sorry," I said.

I slid my hand into my lap and kicked at the porch with the toe of my shoe, setting the rocking chair into motion. Dad and I sat in silence, staring at the yard, as the creaks and squeaks of the rocking chair serenaded us.

Chapter 2

KEVIN

"Twelve doll...dollars even," I said.

"What's that now?" Mrs. Craft cupped her hand to her ear.

"*Tuh-twelve dollars even*," I repeated a little more loudly.

"Twelve dollars, is it?" she tutted. "What about tax now?"

Smiling, I did my best to not become frustrated with Mrs. Craft. We had the same conversation every time she came into the convenience store.

"You only buh-bought unprepared fuh-food, Mrs. Craft," I said loudly enough to be heard by the entire store. "Nothing you bought is tax...taxable."

She frowned at me for a moment, then seemed to accept what I'd said as true—like she had a million other times—before fishing around in her overnight bag-sized purse. Fortunately, mid-afternoons in the store were typically our slowest time of the work day. Waiting for Mrs. Craft to fish out her money wasn't that big of an inconvenience.

Once she'd handed over two fives and two ones, I cashed her out, catching the money drawer with my hip. It had a habit of getting finicky and shooting out of the register and to the floor, spilling its contents in a clattering, jingling mess everywhere. My low-tech, cheap solution was my hip bone.

I added Mrs. Craft's money to the drawer and closed it with a swivel of my hips while simultaneously bagging up her items. Once the bag was transferred across the counter from my hand to hers, she gave me a grunt, turned on her heels, and exited the store.

A gust of hot air, like straight out of an oven, shot through the store, and was only abated by the door swinging shut behind Mrs. Craft. For a moment, I thought I'd get a respite from the unrelenting summer heat. When the door swung open seconds later, and another gust of oven-like air blew through the store, I settled into the fact that it was simply going to be one of those days.

"That woman thinks the sun comes out just to hear her crow. I tell you what."

I smiled at the voice emanating from the front door.

One look confirmed that Wallace Lee was my next customer. Unlike my other customers throughout the day, he was quick to step inside and pull the door shut behind him. Though we both loved summer, the current season was kicking everyone's asses up to around their shoulders. There's summer...and then there's *summer*. The triple digit temps, wrathful sun, and lack of rain was getting to everyone. It was only July.

Scorching summers like the one we were having has one of two effects on people. Either the heat gets to them and they stay angry all season long, ready to fight at the smallest slight, or they get passive and lazy. They wait for the season to peter out so that life can return to some form of normal. Wallace Lee and I were part of a secret third effect group. We did our best to stay positive and happy, knowing that nothing lasts forever. So, seeing Wallace Lee enter the store was a bright spot in my day.

"Mrs. Craft?" I asked in a stage-whisper.

He nodded firmly. Wiped a hand across his brow under the brim of his ball cap.

"Bumped into me comin' out your store," he said, walking over to my register, "and didn't give one damn excuse or apology. Just kept goin'."

Laughing, I said, "That sounds abuh-bout right."

Shaking his head, Wallace Lee pulled his billfold out of the back pocket of his jeans. Small dark circles decorated his shirt near his underarms. The man worked inside an air-conditioned grocery store, so he'd sweated that much in the short walk down the street. He held a ten out to me.

"Pack of Reds," he said.

I frowned at him.

"Ain't gettin' any younger, Kevin," he said. "Give me them Reds."

"I'll guh-ive them to you, but you know you sh...shouldn't smoke, Mister Juh-jones," I said, reaching to the rack hanging over the counter above my head. "They're guh-going to kuh-kill you eventually."

"I'm damn near sixty years old," he said. "What the hell am I holdin' on for?"

Laughing, I took the bill from him and rang him up.

"I duh-don't nuh-know—"

Wallace Lee laid a hand gently on the counter, stopping me.

"Slow down, son," he said gently. "You ain't gotta rush with me."

We exchanged a look and I went about finishing the sale before handing the pack of Marlboros over to him. Wallace Lee accepted them gratefully and immediately began "packing" the cardboard box, pounding the butt of it against the heel of his hand.

"Sorry," I said. "I forget."

"These people around here rush around too much," Wallace Lee shook his head. "Ain't got time to let a fella get the words out his mouth."

Wallace Lee was right. Given time to concentrate and speak slowly, my stutter wasn't as pronounced. Sometimes I didn't stutter at all if I kept calm, concentrated, and spoke at a pace that worked for me.

A bead of sweat trickled down his temple, which he quickly wiped away with the back of his hand.

"Wooooo, boy," he said, peeling the plastic from the box of cigarettes. "It's hotter than two rats screwin' in a wool sock."

I laughed loudly at him as I grabbed the cleaning spray and rag by the register. Often, when Wallace Lee came into the convenience store, and there were no other customers around, he'd stick around. We'd shoot the shit while I wiped down the counters and straightened up. He ran a family-like but tight ship at the grocery store. He could sneak away for a few minutes in the middle of the day to visit without worrying about his store burning down.

"Your family's around the corner there solvin' the world's problems," Wallace Lee slipped the ready pack of cigarettes into the front pocket of his shirt. "Talkin' all kinds of dirt."

"That's no family of mine," I teased back. "I think they duh-descended from some of your ancestors."

He waved me off. "They ain't nearly dark enough. And we've got some characters in our family, but none of 'em are that bad."

Wallace Lee was talking about the old men who had daily meetings at the corner of the convenience store. They'd hang around for hours—even in the blazing sun to talk crap about everyone and everything in town.

"They didn't buh-other you, did they?" I asked as I sprayed down the counter.

"Nah," he said with another wave. "I think they've about given up even lookin' in my direction anymore, to be honest."

"Good."

"I guess if you have to choose between bein' whispered about and bein' ignored, bein' ignored is the best option."

"I guess so."

"They still payin' you in chicken feed around here?" he asked.

I vigorously wiped down the counter with the rag as I smiled over at him.

"Nothing has really chuh-changed, no," I said.

"You shouldn't even be in here doin' this job," Wallace Lee tapped the counter with his finger decisively. "With that fancy business degree you went and got."

I didn't have a response for that logic.

"But if you want to do a workin' man's job, you may as well make as much as you can," he continued. "You know I've always got a job over at the store for you, Kevin."

"I know," I said. "Buh-but Shirley and Ralph were so nuh-nice to hire me anyway. I hate to di-isappoint them."

Wallace Lee waved a hand dismissively again. "They so nice, they'd pay you what you're worth."

Again, his logic couldn't be argued.

"I won't bug you no more today about it," he said. "But I'm sure I'll need another pack of Reds tomorrow."

With that, and my chuckles following him, Wallace Lee made his way to the door. Before swinging the door open to the blistering heat, he turned and gave me a nod.

"Thanks," he said.

"Anytime," I replied.

For the most part, the heat kept everyone home for the rest of the afternoon. After Wallace Lee left, I spent the last two hours of my shift cleaning the store from top to bottom. Small town; small convenience store. It didn't take much effort or time to have it sparkling clean.

By the time Danielle came in to take over for the late afternoon and evening shift, there wasn't much left for her to do besides wait behind the register. Not that having nothing to do at work is a real problem. We said our "hellos" and a few other pleasantries before I clocked out and headed out for the day.

Living in a small town for my entire life—save the four years in Austin for college—I'd never seen the need for a car. You can walk from one end of town to the other in less than ten minutes, and there's not much to walk to, anyway. We have the Sav-A-Ton, where everyone gets their groceries if they don't drive out to the big Wal-Mart in the next town over. There's Carla Rae's Café, where everyone goes to eat if they don't drive out of town. And then we have the convenience store-slash-gas station, which is where I work.

There are a few small shops, an insurance agency, a tiny bank, and a beauty salon on the main street, but that's about it. The longest walk in town is for the kids who wander out into the woods to hang out at the creek. Even a walk from the far end of the town to the creek takes less than fifteen minutes. I used to go to the creek a lot when it was age appropriate. Now, I only go every once in a while, to see how it's holding up. Of course, you can't drive down to the creek, so, again, I've never had a reason for a car.

Walking to the creek was what I decided to do after leaving the convenience store. Lately, due to the drought and the creek drying up, I'd been visiting more often. A miraculous recovery, showing up to find it full of crystal clear, cool water once again, wasn't going to happen. So, I wasn't entirely certain why I kept going out there with any semblance of hope.

Of course, in the back of my mind, I knew of one reason. From time to time, if I showed up at the right moment in the day, I'd run into him. Carson.

I'd promised Mike and Ian before they left for New York that I'd be there for Carson if he needed anything. They'd said they would let Carson know. Ian had personally insinuated that I should insert myself in Carson life as much as I could. Let him know I was there in such a way that he could never forget. A month had passed since they left, the creek had run dry, and Carson hadn't called once. And he hadn't taken the bait when I did my best to initiate interaction.

Seeing me at the creek by chance, even though it was dried up, might have spurred Carson into action. That had been my hope. Every time I put myself in his path, he pretended to not see me. Or he'd see me, but he wouldn't acknowledge me.

I didn't know what hurt worse. Being ignored by Carson.

Or being ignored and knowing that he had no right to my kindness.

He'd treated me like a bug under his foot for the first few years of high school. Carson and his buddies had terrorized me, and, if not for Ian, might have done worse. Yet I was offering to be there for him now that we were adults. And he was pretending I didn't exist.

When I found myself out at the creek, staring across the dry gulch at Carson, I wasn't going to say or do anything. But I found myself giving him a small smile and a wave. He stared at me blankly, turned, and walked away. Not a single word, action, or facial expression to acknowledge me.

Overcome with unreasonable frustration, I thought about picking up a rock. Chucking it across the creek at him. Maybe my aim would be good enough to peg him in the back. Or the back of his head. The anger was fleeting, however, and I simply watched him disappear back into the woods on his side of the creek.

So, with a sigh, I shuffled home. The dry leaves poked at my skin through my socks and the exigent silence filled my ears the entire way.

Once I was back in town, walking along the side of the main street on my way home, I couldn't shake Carson from my mind. He said nothing. He didn't even smile. His face was blank every time I happened to run across him. It was that blankness, the hollow look in his eyes, the obvious, intentional way he controlled his emotions, that I couldn't forget.

He looked haunted.

As though he was slowly disappearing, fading to a whisper of himself. A foggy mist that would one day be carried away by the warm Texas breeze.

All he needed was a sheet and a chain to no longer be haunted, but instead, become another thing that haunted our town. He'd stay alive in the whispers and murmurs of the townies for a time—especially the old men who met every day at the coffee shop. Until that too became old news and even his memory would be dead.

Carson, as I knew him, and what he came to be, would end up having barely existed. There would come a day that I would mention his name, and the person would respond: "*Oh, yeah. I kinda remember that guy. Tall, right?*"

I suppose that is what we're moving toward in life— becoming a piece of the hazy collective memory of the people who knew us least and haunting the memories of those who can't forget us.

Like memories of past summers in the creek.

We'll all be a slash of a wound on the landscape of human existence one day. A vague memory too ugly and useless to stay relevant to people's every day existence.

My parents' house is in the "rich part" of town. If there is such a thing. There's not much town to really divide it into the "haves" and "have nots," though there are plenty of "have nots" and few "haves." The house, located on the one street in town whose tress still have green leaves and whose lawns are still lush and emerald, is nice compared to everything else in town.

Going home at the end of a shift at the store is a chore. The quiet disapproval of my parents' gaze, the silent judgment of my life choices, the unspoken belief that my brother before me has achieved much more, is a weight crushing my chest. I can forget it during the hours I'm at work, but never at home. Not even when I'm locked up in my room all alone.

Jogging around the side of the house, I smiled at the thought that if I slipped into the house through the back door, I could avoid my parents. I'd take the back stairs off the kitchen hallway. Interacting with them and enduring their silent disapproval could be avoided until dinner time.

Then again, maybe I wouldn't be all that hungry and I could avoid them at dinner, too.

Once they were in bed I could slip down to the kitchen and pilfer leftovers from the fridge. Or bake a frozen pizza or something. Anything to avoid the torment that is being twenty-two years old and living with one's parents.

As I made my way up the back stairs, stepping lightly on the wood slats to avoid detection, I grinned at my plan. The Four

O'Clocks in the flower beds alongside the stairs were beginning their late day blooming. The drought would have had its way with them, but like all of the other people on our street, my parents were not against ignoring the town's water ban. The flowers stood proudly in their wasted existence.

I'd barely placed my hand on the door handle when I first heard the voices. Grimacing, I realized that Mom and Dad were in the kitchen. Probably sitting around the table, having an afternoon coffee, and catching up on their days.

My first instinct was to creep back down the stairs and around to the front door. Slipping in the front door and up the front stairs might be possible. Sweat was trickling down between my shoulder blades and I wanted to be up in my room, on my bed, under the fan. However, before I could let go of the doorhandle, my parents' voices reached my ears.

"...*just sits up in his room all night.*"

"*Well—*"

"*He only gets out to go to that damned store, Patricia. He's doing nothing.*"

"*We should give him time. He's only twenty-two.*"

"*Oh, psh. Mark had a decent job lined up right after college. If you're going to baby Kevin, I don't even want to talk about it. Kevin has no ambition—wasting everything we've provided for him. He's becoming a waste of space.*"

Emotionlessly, I let go of the door handle. And I backed down the stairs silently.

I didn't sneak around to the front door and up the front staircase to my room.

With my head hung, and doing my best to feel nothing, I shuffled across the yard in the hazy late afternoon sun to the edge of the yard. I flung myself down under the old Live Oak, putting my back to the trunk.

I'd sneak upstairs when they were getting ready for bed.

Chapter 3
CARSON

He followed me to the creek.

Sara Lee coming by and hanging out every day with Dad was a blessing and a curse. It was helpful so that I could get away from the house for a little bit each day. I could do chores and run errands and pick up odd jobs here and there.

Putting up with Sara Lee's savior complex was one of the downsides.

And having more free time to myself meant there were more opportunities for Kevin to run into me. However, I couldn't just hang around the house with Dad and Sara Lee. She'd get on my nerves, ask too many questions, tell me to get out of the house for a bit. Avoiding Kevin became impossible if I couldn't hide away.

I'm not stupid.

A lot of people think I am. Or have thought so at one point or another. Big dumb-dumb ex-high school bully who lives out on the edge of town with his disabled father. Poor white trash. Barely graduated high school.

Surprised he didn't turn out worse or get worse, honestly.

You know his mother's dead 'cause of his old man, don't you? Let me tell you all about it...

I know who whispers and what they whisper.

And I don't blame them.

But I'm not dumb.

Especially when it came to Kevin. Even if Ian and Mike hadn't stopped by on their way out of town with their bags of pity groceries—*not that I wasn't grateful*—I knew Kevin was tight with the two of them. I knew they all went to the same college and were probably thick as thieves for all four years. So, the look in Kevin's eyes every time he saw me was transparent.

Look after the big dumb-dumb ex-high school bully, wouldja?

That knowledge hurt somewhere deep inside of me that didn't even have a name. Especially since I'd earned no kindness.

I find scorn and indifference easier to accept than kindness anymore.

Hurts less than kindness, anyway. It's a dull ache compared to a sharp stab.

I ignored him when he followed me to the creek. Kevin stayed several steps back, trailing along behind me through the woods, making his presence known. He said nothing, though. I wanted to tell him that saying nothing while following me was creepy and not having the desired effect.

That would have encouraged him, me speaking to him.

If I ignored him long enough, he'd eventually give up. He'd drift away like everyone else in my life and leave me to my shack, my disabled father, and my solitary existence.

So, after I checked out the creek, I turned and walked right past him without uttering a word. He didn't follow me out of the woods. My message had been received. At least for that day.

The following day was the same. And the next. Kevin followed me to the woods, stood along the bank, further down the creek, looked down at the dusty gulch as I did, and then I turned and left him there. A week went by of having my own personal shadow follow me out to the creek.

Kevin refused to take the hint, but stubbornly said nothing to me. He was waiting for me to speak first, which really pissed me off.

He was trying to be kind.

On a Sunday, when Sara Lee had come by after church to sit with Dad and prepare a big Sunday supper for all of us, I decided to take the time it would take her to cook and stretch my legs. It was as if Kevin had planted a homing beacon on me. I'd barely gotten to the edge of the woods when he fell in step behind me.

Leaves crunched under our feet as we made our way through the brown, forgotten woods. Twigs snapped underfoot and the silence that only a dying land can make blanketed us the entire way.

As was typical, we stood on the bank of the creek and stared down at the dried creek bed. The dried slashes in the dirt were like mouths screaming up to the heavens for relief. The sky has no ears and the ground has no voice, so the pleas would be unheard and unheeded. For how long, I had no idea.

Kevin stood ten feet down shore from me, but for once, he wasn't staring down at the dried valley carving its way through the woods. He was watching me. Not out of the corner of his eye. No subtle glances or sneakiness. He was *staring* at me.

Turning to leave, I realized that Kevin could go on like this forever. I wasn't certain that I could continue putting up with his kindness. I found myself drawing on experience.

If you make them hate you, they'll leave you alone.

When Kevin fell in behind me, I turned to face him. He skidded to a stop, nearly running into me since he hadn't expected my actions. I didn't look around him or through him. I locked eyes with him. Though I didn't have the energy to put any real emotion into my words, I finally said something to Kevin after more than a week of having him shadow me.

"*Leave me alone,*" I hissed. "*Faggot.*"

Kevin's eyes seemed to well up, but it wasn't with unshed tears. He was hurt, but not by my words. Not by me. The hurt was something deeper.

It was pity.

So, I shoved him. Though I couldn't put much effort into that action, either.

He stumbled, but his expression didn't change. So, I shoved him again.

"*Stop following me, faggot!*" I managed to growl.

My expectation was that Kevin would be scared or hurt enough to finally decide to leave me be. That if I turned and walked away, he wouldn't follow. And the next day he wouldn't fall in behind me as I made my way out to the woods again.

Kevin's fist clocking me sharply in the chin was unexpected.

Stunned at first, I could only stare at him. When he swung again, the second punch landing against my cheek, I took a step back as my head whipped to the side. A third punch caught me in the shoulder. A fourth in the nose. Viscous, searing hot blood welled and dripped from my nose and into the back of my throat immediately.

"*Do suh…something!*" Kevin howled at me. "*Say something!*"

The next punch caught me on the chin again.

"*What the hell is ruh-wrong with you?*" Kevin growled, his voice cracking.

The next punch I dodged. Not because I didn't think I deserved it, but because I was getting tired of being hit. I barely had time to spit out the blood pooling at the back of my throat when Kevin began to swing wildly. I was too tired to dodge any punches he threw after the first four. So, I threw one back.

Connecting with the tip of Kevin's chin, I barely cracked him, but it was enough to get his attention. It made him stop swinging as he stumbled back in shock.

When his feet found purchase and he righted himself, he stared at me angrily. This time, the water in his eyes wasn't pity. But it wasn't quite anger, either. I spat again, a crimson streak splattering the brown leaves at my feet, but my eyes didn't move from Kevin's.

Finally, after leaving to me to wonder for far too long about whether or not he'd swing at me again, Kevin rushed past me. His shoulder bumped mine violently as he went by.

"*Fuck you*," he muttered.

For God knows how long I stood there, listening to the leaves and twigs crackle under his feet as he marched out of the woods. Finally, silence pervaded once more.

I licked the blood from my teeth. Rubbed my chin.

And managed a ghost of a smile.

Who knew he had it in him?

Chapter 4

KEVIN

Faint buzzing drew my attention the following day on my walk home from work. Not wanting to go home had led me into cyclic thoughts about how I could avoid it. A strange buzzing, almost like swarming bees, was as good a reason as any to make a detour. That I walked towards the sound of potentially swarming bees underlined how desperately I didn't want to go home.

I hadn't been aware that I was walking by Wallace Lee's house when I'd heard the noise, but following the noise, I quickly came to realize where I was. Rounding the white clapboard house, with the white picket fence that enclosed the front lawn, I made my way to the field-like backyard.

Wallace Lee's property stretched from the back of his small, but beautiful home all the way to the edge of the woods, nearly fifty yards away. As I walked along the side of the house, with a clear view of the woods in the distance, people in strange white outfits were doing something along the tree line. The woods were brown and the trees looked skeletal in the distance. I crept along the side of the house, wondering if I wasn't intruding on something that was none of my business.

At the corner of the backside of the house, I stood silently and tried to make out what the people at the edge of the woods were doing. They looked as if they were wearing oversized white jumpsuits and boots and gloves. The hats with what looked like veils hanging down to cover their faces should have tipped me off. If I'd had enough time, I might have figured things out on my own. A voice to my right saved me from having to think too hard.

"Beekeepers," Wallace Lee said.

I turned my head to find him sitting in an old green and white cantilever clamshell metal patio chair. He had a beer in one hand and his legs were kicked out and crossed before him. A smoldering cigarette dangled from his lips as he stared out at the woods beyond his property.

"Wuh-what?"

"Beekeepers, son," he said with a chuckle, though he still didn't turn to look at me. "Kids up from the college."

I turned to look out at the people by the woods.

"They done found a colony of bees out yunder," he said. "This drought's gonna do 'em no good. They asked if they could set up a hive out there at the end of my property line. I figured why not, you know?"

"Yeah."

"They're havin' a helluva time of it, though." Wallace Lee chuckled, coughed, took a drag from his smoke and a sip from his beer. "Them bees don't want to behave."

I stared out at the beekeepers in their strange garb, the buzzing of what was likely hundreds—or even thousands—of bees in the distance.

"I guess no one likes being told what to do," I said.

"Never a truth better told," Wallace Lee said, stretching languidly in his chair as he watched the beekeepers work. "They just want to collect their pollen and make their honey and serve the queen, I imagine. Then they got these folks up in their business tellin' what to do and where to do it."

I laughed lightly.

"They're tryin' to get them all into that makeshift hive there," he continued, "and they've brought in some mobile garden with all kinds of flowers. Put it out there just beyond the trees. Gives the bees something to do—a way to collect their pollen and make their honey. They come out and water it every few days. This damn drought, you know?"

I nodded, though I wasn't sure if Wallace Lee was actually looking at me.

"You know it takes ten pounds of pollen to make one pound of honey?" he asked suddenly.

"No."

"Learned that from those kids. Damn somethin', ain't it?" he asked. "Who'd have thought that bees have to work that hard to do the one thing they live to do? You'd think the things would be happy to have the process streamlined for 'em, but they just ain't takin' to it like you'd think. They want to fly all over the woods and choose for themselves which flowers and plants to visit. They want to live in the hive they made, not some box."

"Makes sense, I guess," I said.

"They told me—the beekeepers, not the bees—," he chuckled, "—that usually, bees don't give them this much trouble. It's usually a lot easier to get them to join the new hives they build and all that."

"Yeah?"

"I told them they just ain't met these kinds of bees before. These bees up here are feisty. Not like them educated bees down by the college. Those bees are sophisticated. We got wild ones up here."

We both laughed.

"I'm sure they loved that," I said, turning to face Wallace Lee.

He was watching me.

"Might be farfetched but it's proven true so far," he said quietly, staring at me.

For some reason, I felt self-conscious. Wallace Lee seemed to be staring into my soul.

"Angry bruise you got there," he said.

He jabbed at his chin with a finger. Automatically, my hand went to my chin. I winced when my fingertips touched the tender blue and purple flesh.

"Yeah," I said, averting my eyes as I rubbed the sore spot.

"Saw another boy this morning," Wallace Lee said smoothly, "bit bruised up as well."

I said nothing, but my hand fell from my chin. Turning to look at the beekeepers again, I felt sad. Wallace Lee and I watched the bees and their keepers in communal silence for a few moments before he spoke again.

"Some things just don't want to be told what to do," Wallace Lee reiterated my point. "Sometimes you gotta coax 'em. Have the patience of a saint. Those bees will come 'round eventually. Especially once they realize the hive and the mobile garden are a sight better than nothin'."

"Yeah."

"Once they figure out it's feast or famine, they'll choose the feast."

I thought about that.

"Wuh-what if they don't mind stuh-starving…if it means they'll get their way? Is anything that stuh-stubborn?"

He chuckled. "Some things have sawdust for brains, for sure. The bees and the other wild things ain't one of 'em. They ain't survived this long by being stupid."

I sighed.

"I've probably had too many, but you want a beer?" he asked. "You're old enough, right?"

"Yeah," I said. "No. I…I have to get home. Dinner. With Mom and Dad?"

I would have loved to stay and sit with Wallace Lee. Talk about bees—though I was certain Wallace Lee wasn't talking about bees—but I felt too seen. Exposed.

"All right then," he said. "Tell your mom and dad I said 'hello' for me."

I turned to look at him.

"For what it's worth," he said with a small smile as he tipped his beer at me.

Wallace Lee didn't know my parents all that well. They didn't know him all that well. And we both knew my parents weren't much better than the old men who hung around in the coffee shop and by the old crates outside the convenience store. He was kind enough to not say as much.

I found myself wondering what kindness costs certain people. Day in and day out, some people must be suffocated by their own kindness in a world that sees it as weakness. Yet they continue being kind, suffocated.

"Okay."

Chapter 5

CARSON

He didn't follow me to the creek the next day. I didn't see Kevin at all the following day. When I got out to the creek, he was nowhere to be found. He wasn't hiding behind the trees, watching me or standing on the other side of the creek, keeping his distance. Kevin had given up. A small, bitter smile graced my lips as a hollow feeling prickled at the sides of my gut.

I tried not to think about it.

I'd made my point and gotten my way. There was nothing to think about anyway.

When I returned to the house after not finding Kevin waiting for me, I had dinner with Sara Lee and Dad. Went through my nightly routine of getting Dad ready for sleep. Saw Sara Lee off for the evening. Washed up and went to bed.

I rarely stay up late since Dad wakes up pretty early each day and I have to get up and help him through the morning routines until Sara Lee shows up. That night, however, I found myself restless. Tossing and turning under the covers, the scratchy sheet tore across my legs like a cheese grater. The oppressive heat made my skin feel sticky.

Frantically kicking off the covers, annoyed with the heat keeping me awake, I'd pushed my boxers down to mid-thigh. And I did the one thing that unfailingly put me to sleep. However, afterwards, I'd only managed to make myself hotter, stickier, and more frustrated. Uncertain when I actually drifted off, because it did eventually happened, when my eyes popped open again after the sun rose, I wasn't any less tense than the night before.

The creek was lonely that afternoon as well. With no rain in sight, the kids in town were steering clear of the woods, and without Kevin following me, my daily trip into the woods was silent. No birds chirping, no animals scurrying, no breeze to speak of, and no trickling of running water gave the woods an eerie, deathly feel.

Leaves crunching underfoot sounded like otherworldly whispers.

After the first day of going out to the creek and finding it— and everything around it—barren and lonely, I realized that I'd managed to scare off Kevin. As I stood at the edge of the creek, staring down at the dry, deeply cracked earth below, I wasn't certain I felt accomplished. Though I felt that it was for the best.

It brought me no comfort.

That night, lying in bed, a sheen of sweat on my skin and the sheets and my boxers down around my ankles again, my attempt to ease myself into sleep felt violent. Angry and desperate, an ache in my gut that I couldn't quite understand, I glared up at the ceiling through eyes stinging from the drops of sweat that dribbled down my brow and into them.

Sometimes, my body feels like a pressure cooker and my dick is the vent pipe. Pressure has to be released so that I don't explode. Masturbation can be pleasurable, but more than anything, it's utilitarian. It's a release at the end of another day that was like the thousands that came before it. A method of resetting myself so that when more pressure inevitably builds the next day, I don't explode.

It was the only method I had anymore. To relieve the daily pressure that life imposed.

When I went out to the creek the following day, I didn't stroll down the path that I'd come to know like the back of my hand. I marched. Stomped. The brown and dying leaves and skeletal twigs were my enemies and my feet were my army. The woods knew my frustration by the sounds of my feet grinding my enemies into the dirt in the path before me.

If any birds and critters were hiding in the woods, my march down the trail would have surely scared them off. Like every other day before that summer, I heard nothing other than the ground underfoot and the snorting of angry breaths from my nose. The bruises on my face—which Sara Lee hadn't even asked about—had settled into greenish-yellow spots, tender to the touch, but easily ignored if I kept my hands from my face.

When I exited the woods into the creek clearing that wound its way through the woods, I nearly tripped over my own feet and tumbled into the dry creek bed below. Kevin wasn't waiting in the usual spot where we would check out the creek. But he was there. On the other side.

He was sitting on the bank, one knee pulled up to his chest. He was looking down at his hand, running something through his fingers. Considering it with the eyes of a curious scholar. He didn't look up at me, though I knew he had heard me stomping all the way from town into the woods. Anything within a mile would have heard me coming.

So, I looked down at the creek as though I would find anything new. As though it had miraculously rained overnight and I had simply missed it. I'd slept so lightly that a mist against the roof of our shack would have woken me. I hadn't missed any rain. There was no point in staring down at the gulch any longer.

I meant to turn and leave, stomp back the way I'd come. But I couldn't. I was tired. I wanted to be annoyed and angry and frustrated and…I was tired. So, with a glance over at Kevin once more—he was still staring at whatever he was running between his fingers—I lowered myself to the ground.

Craggy earth and hay-like grass met my hands and backside as I settled into my spot. I pulled my knees up to my chest and wrapped my arms around them, my eyes fixed on the empty creek before me. It was silent. The woods…maybe they were dead?

Had the drought finally accomplished its task?

I would have given anything for a breeze, no matter how arid, to whistle through the clearing. Or for a cricket to chirp. A twig to crack in the distance. There was nothing but overwhelming silence. It was unnerving.

"Do you thuh-think," Kevin practically whispered, barely audible in the space the dusty gulch put between us, "that when it finally ruh-rains, it'll make a difference?"

Slowly, I raised my head to look at him.

He was still looking down at his hand, avoiding my eyes.

When I said nothing, he continued.

"Is the cuh…reek done?" he asked, though I wasn't sure who he was asking. "It's huh-hard to look at it and even ruh-remember swimming here. You nuh-know?"

I let him sit with his thoughts as I stared at him. Finally, his fingers opened, and a piece of straw-like grass fluttered to the ground before him. He looked sad.

We sat in silence for…I wasn't sure how long. The woods and the creek offered no soundtrack to our actions.

"When it rains," I found myself saying back softly, though my voice sounded hoarse, "I hope it's not a lot."

Finally, Kevin looked up at me, a confused look on his face.

"Too much rain at once after a long drought is never good," I explained. "The ground's too dry. It won't be able to soak up the rain that quickly. It can be dangerous."

Kevin continued to stare at me.

"We'll need several days of steady rain to fix this." I gave a small nod to the creek.

Finally, a ghost of a smile passed across Kevin's face.

"Wonder huh-how luh-long we'll have to wait."

I started to shrug, but I was too tired.

"Weathermen don't seem to know," I said. "I guess we have to wait and find out."

The smile tugged at the corner of Kevin's mouth.

"Sorry I hit you," he said.

I did shrug then.

"I probably deserved to be hit."

"Nobody duh-deserves to be huh-hit," Kevin said, looking away. "Nothing duh-deserves to feel that way."

I didn't tell him that I didn't need his help to feel any certain way. I didn't tell him anything. We sat across the creek from each other and stared down into the empty crevice. It had been mid-afternoon when I'd ventured into the woods. The sun was beginning to kiss the horizon when the two of us stood without saying a word and stared at each other from across the creek.

"Maybe tomorrow?" Kevin said.

I nodded. That whisper of a smile appeared, disappeared, and then he nodded. We headed off in opposite directions.

A week went by and every day was the same. Kevin was sitting on the opposite side of the creek when I arrived each afternoon. I'd sit down and we'd exchange a few words. Wait for the sun to announce it was time to leave. And we'd leave the woods in opposite directions. Each day we talked about the rain that had to come. *Didn't it?* But the creek was still dry when we headed home each day.

However, sleep didn't elude me each night. When I pushed the sheets and my boxers down to down my legs each night, it didn't feel perfunctory. And as each day passed, I showed up at the creek better rested.

Chapter 6

KEVIN

"How l…ong can this go on?" I asked.

I was mostly talking to myself. The ground was so parched it seemed to creak under my weight as I sat there on the bank of the dried-up creek. The grass—if it could even be called that anymore—snapped like glass with each movement against it. The earth felt dead. Sitting there on the baked clay that was the creek bank made it feel as though it might collapse, crumble, and toss me into the arid gulch below at any moment.

After another week of triple-digit temperatures and not a single drop of rain, I couldn't help but believe that our new way of life was permanent.

"The old-timers keep talking about some drought that happened thirty years ago," Carson murmured, glancing at me, but not maintaining eye contact. "They say it went on for two seasons."

"Shit."

"Shit," he agreed.

For a few more moments we sat there. The hazy yellow light of the sun baking our skin and somehow making the world look even more brown and lifeless.

"They're h…aving to ruh-replace the air conditioner at the store," I said, apropos nothing. "It was already a puh-piece of crap. It was puh-probably a huh-undred years old already. This huh-eat was the fuh-final nail in the coffin."

Carson smiled but he still didn't meet my eyes.

"I swear I swuh-weated through my jeans today," I said, chuckling lightly.

"The house is like that," Carson said, then seemed to realize what he said. "Yeah. It's hot."

I wanted to ask Carson if they had air conditioning at his house, but I knew the answer. Offering help of some kind was my next thought, but I'd only recently gotten him to actually talk to me. Showing any sign of pity would shut him down again.

"Do you have any fuh-fans?" I asked.

"We're fine," he grumbled.

I said nothing in response. He took a measured breath.

"Yeah," he said. "We're good. We'll be fine."

Nodding, I wasn't sure if he noticed my silent response.

Though Carson hadn't become effusive in his displays of fellowship over the last few weeks, we were spending longer stretches of time at the creek when I finished my shift at the store each day. Some nights, the moon was coming out when we went our separate ways. I wanted to ask Carson how he was able to spend so much time out at the creek each day, since his father wasn't well, but I knew that question wouldn't be received well, either. I decided that it was best to assume he had some system to make sure his dad was looked after.

"Do you," Carson began, then stopped.

Looking across the gulch at him, I waited. Carson was not the type of person you forced into speaking.

"Feels like the woods are in mourning," he said finally. "That's all."

"Mourning?" I asked.

He shrugged. "Like they're missing something."

"I nuh..know what 'muh-muh-mourning' means, jackass," I said, hoping Carson would receive it well.

He smiled faintly. So, I smiled back, though he was still avoiding my eyes.

"The creek has never gone dry in my lifetime," Carson said. "Especially not in the last ten years. I'm just wondering. You know?"

Drawn from examining Carson, I looked around at the barren woods cast in sepia and the hazy gold light that burned my eyes. I felt of the ground at my sides, felt the cracks and crevices and the sharp blades of grass against the flesh of my palms. I did know what Carson meant. I'd wondered the same thing myself, though, like Carson, I had to wonder if it was a ridiculous thought.

How can the earth mourn?

"They didn't even nuh-know how much they were nuh-oticed, did they?" I found myself whispering.

Carson glanced up at me.

"It was like," I sighed, pulled my knees to my chest, "I don't know. I guh-guess sometimes people don't ruh...ealize how much other puh-people are wuh-watching them. They were a fixture. If Ian and Mike were in the wuh-woods, it was...I don't know. Things were complete?"

Carson hadn't averted his eyes, but his brow had furrowed, and his eyes seemed to be glazed over.

"Like, when you puh...ull the puh-plug out of the tub and everything drains," I said quietly. "They were as much a part of these woods as the trees and the cuh-creek and the squirrels."

He nodded, still gazing out at nothing.

"That's weird, right?" I asked.

Carson shrugged and his eyes refocused.

47

"I hated them, you know?"

He had spoken so clearly so suddenly, that it startled me. I didn't respond.

"I mean," he looked down at the ground, "not really. Not completely. They…I didn't know…*everything*…that was going on with them. Not right away. I just knew they had each other. Best buds. They weren't alone. Like the rest of us."

Nodding, the corner of my mouth turned up.

"*Best buds*," I parroted.

Carson glanced at me and we both blushed; grinned.

"The woods loved them," Carson said. He was talking more in the last few minutes than he had in an entire two weeks. "It was their…thing. I hated them for that. Kind of."

"I huh-hated them, too," I admitted. "Because they had each other. They're my buh-best friends now, though. So, I guess I never huh…ated them. Not really."

"Sounds like we were paying too much attention."

I laughed. "Probably."

"Why are you being nice to me?" Carson asked suddenly.

I cocked my head to the side and stared at him.

"You should hate me, too," he said.

"I don't."

"Why not?"

I thought about that for a moment as we stared at each other.

"I guess I kind of did," I said, unable to not grin a little. "Buh…but only for a little bit."

He grinned sheepishly and looked down; his cheeks were rosy.

"Ian tuh-told me once," I began, "that survival ruh-required ruthlessness. Living required kindness."

Carson watched me for a moment. "Yeah?"

"I guh...uess I realized you were surviving," I said. "And I decided I wanted to live."

Carson said nothing, but I was certain he agreed. We sat in silence for a long time, until the sun was dipping below the horizon. Finally, we both stood, brushed off the seats of our jeans, and looked at each other from across the creek.

"Maybe tomorrow?" Carson said, just as we'd been saying for two weeks.

"Maybe tomorrow." I nodded.

And we went our separate ways.

As I sauntered out of the woods under the lingering rays of the oppressive sun, I felt light somehow. Even the drought-stricken woods couldn't ruin my mood. There had been so many things I wanted to ask Carson. About his life. How he was doing. I wanted to offer him help or at least an ear for his problems. He had plenty. But I knew that bringing up anything about his life would set me back in trying to become friends with him. If things had to continue the way they were going— even for years—I'd keep at it. Eventually, he'd come around. He was already talking to me more, so that was promising.

Halfway home, as I was walking by Wallace Lee's place, the buzzing of bees reached my ears, and I automatically smiled. I had no idea why. I'd never given a crap about bees. I loved honey, but I'd never considered that honey required bees. Instead of carrying on home, I found myself walking around the edge of Wallace Lee's house, venturing into the backyard again.

As it had been a few weeks before, I found him sitting in his metal clamshell lawn chair, staring out at the far end of his property. A glance in that direction let me know that the beekeepers were nowhere to be found. The bees sounded riled up, though. Stopping at the corner of his house, I didn't get a chance to speak before Wallace Lee noticed me.

"Another hot one," he said, raising a beer to his lips before taking a slug.

"Yeah."

"The bees aren't happy about it."

"I cuh-can see—*hear*—that," I said with a chuckle.

"Those students were out here earlier," he said. "They said the bees are still being stubborn about that mobile garden."

"What are they guh…oing to do?" I asked.

"The bees? Hell if I know. They're stubborn as all get out."

I laughed again. "No. The buh-beekeepers. Can't they…*do suh…omething?*"

"Well," Wallace Lee turned his gaze from me to look out at the bees swarming at the edge of the woods by the makeshift hive, "they said they think the bees aren't settling in and doing what they want because they still want to take care of their hive. Probably still full of honey or somethin'. They're just trying to do what's natural to 'em."

"Oh."

"Yeah," he said, sipping his beer again. "I suspect they're going to try to find their hive. Maybe move the honey to the new hive? Destroy it? Hell if I know. They better do something if they ever want these things to settle down."

"Do you—"

"Don't go out there," Wallace Lee warned me suddenly. "They're feisty."

"I'm definitely not guh-going to duh-do that," I said with a nervous chuckle. "I was juh…ust wondering how they're guh-going to find their old hive."

He shrugged and sipped his beer. "Between you, me, and the fencepost, these kids from up the college don't know anything about country livin'. They only understand bees from a textbook."

I nodded.

"Then again," he said with a smile, "I don't know shit-all about bees, either. So, I can't really dog them too much about their lack of progress."

"I guess we'll keep wuh…aiting," I said, looking up at the darkening, cloudless sky.

"Sometimes that's all you can do," Wallace Lee agreed. "I'm betting the bees will figure it out if we give them time."

CARSON

Two grocery bags from Sav-A-Ton were dangling from my fingers. All I could do was stare at Dad. Sara Lee was making him as comfortable as possible, but there was never perfection when it came to Dad's comfort. His skin was nearly as white as the plastic bags holding our groceries, and the veins in his eyes were as red as the Sav-A-Ton logo stamped on their sides.

"I'm afraid so," Sara Lee said, responding to the only question I'd been able to ask.

Is he sure?

"Doc Marshall says so, anyway," Sara Lee murmured as she rose from her stooped position and stood to look down at Dad. His head was laid back against the headrest, his mouth was slightly open, and his eyes drooped lazily. "Says we're gettin' to the end now."

I stared at Dad.

The end.

"I guess we shouldn't be too shocked and all," Sara Lee continued, lacing her arms over her chest. "Was bound to come sooner or later."

I breathed. Took another breath. My gaze didn't avert from Dad's ghostly face. Maybe Dr. Marshall, Dad's primary care physician through the VA, was right about the end. The way Dad looked, I had to imagine that his timeline wasn't off.

The end was here.

Since my mom and dad got into their car wreck, and Dad was confined to his chair, I suppose I'd always imagined there would be an end. At first, each day felt like the end. When you're fourteen, you can't imagine the once strong and healthy man you knew as your father could last long, confined to a wheelchair, unable to speak, rarely able to move, unable to eat on his own. You imagine that, surely, death will come within days. Because, when you're young and healthy, you can't imagine that anything but young and healthy can last for long.

I'd been wrong. Dad had lasted through high school. Another year. Another. It was six years after high school—a decade since the wreck—and he'd held on. There hadn't been a weak person in that chair for those ten years. He'd held on like a champ.

Now he was tired. Spent.

And I found myself realizing, after convincing myself for over a decade that he'd last forever, that I was going to be forced to let him go.

I breathed.

"Well," Sara Lee sighed, "did you get all your shoppin' done?"

I squeezed my fists around the plastic handles of the bags. "Yeah."

"Give those here," Sara Lee said, reaching out. "I'll get dinner started."

Unsure of how to let go of the bags, Sara Lee ended up prying the bags from my hands gently and carrying them over to the small, pitiful aluminum and Formica table in the small and pitiful kitchen. I continued to stare down at Dad.

"Hon," Sara Lee stepped between Dad and me and cautiously laid her hands on my shoulders, "maybe you should go on one of your walks? Ya' think?"

Not looking at her, I somehow remembered to nod. Unable to turn around, Sara Lee's hands guided me. She spun me around and gave me a small nudge towards the door. My feet shifted into autopilot as she patted my shoulder.

"Dinner will be ready whenever you get back," she said softly. "I'll keep a plate warm for you. Stay with your dad until you get back. All right?"

I nodded.

Typically, my feet would have carried me to the creek. The one safe place in my entire world. When I found them shuffling across the threshold of the Sav-A-Ton—for the second time in an hour—I wasn't sure where I was being led. Or why. Moments later, I found myself standing behind Wallace Lee as he stocked vegetables in the produce section. I said nothing, but something must have let him know that I was standing there like a weirdo, watching him. He glanced casually over his shoulder, as though sensing someone was there, jolted, then smiled.

He had opened his mouth to say something, but my voice stopped him.

"Dad's dying," I said robotically, not really seeing Wallace Lee. "I'll need a job. I'll need something besides sweeping floors for groceries."

Wallace Lee stared at me; his expression blank as he considered me. I knew he was considering if showing sympathy would be well received. Finally, after what seemed like forever, and I was certain that I would fall apart right there among the fruits and vegetables of our tiny town's grocery store, he nodded at me, his expression unchanged.

"You let me know when you're ready to start," he said. "I'll have a job for you."

I returned his nod, turned, and walked away. Wallace Lee said something as I left, though my ears felt like they were full of cotton. He had probably said "goodbye" or something similar. I hoped he hadn't said "I'm sorry." I had no use for "sorry."

With my most important mission accomplished, my feet finally delivered me to the creek. Walking up to the edge of the bank of the creek, I stared out at nothing. I didn't look down at the dry, cracked earth at the bottom of the gulch or the reedy straws of grass that seemed to stick out everywhere. There was no point. The woods were dead. The creek was dry. There'd been no rain.

There was no hope.

I found myself wondering how a person can feel empty enough to float away but also as though they're being tugged into the earth by a rope attached to their gut. How can someone feel heavy and weightless all at the same time?

Uncertain how long I stood at the side of the creek, I was also uncertain why I hadn't heard Kevin's footsteps along the path through the woods. Even when he suddenly appeared out of nowhere in the corner of my vision, it didn't startle me. He smiled at me and spoke, but my ears still felt like they were full of cotton. His words sounded like whale calls under water.

Of course, when I didn't respond, his smile slid from his face, replaced with a concerned expression. More words came from him—I knew because I could see his mouth moving in the corner of my eye—but they failed to find my ears as well.

When he reached out tentatively, and his fingers brushed my elbow, I could hear again. It wasn't the muffled sounds of the woods, nor the sound of Kevin's voice, which flooded my ears. It was the thrumming of my pulse. The rush of angry blood circulating my body at twice its normal speed.

The growl of fury that rose from somewhere deep inside of me filled in the spaces between the thrums of my pulse. I have no idea what I grabbed or where I found the things in my hands, but I was suddenly throwing things into the creek.

Rocks.

I think rocks.

My fingers were scratching at the ground, searching for anything to hurl into the craggy abyss below. Kevin's words sounded like they were coming from underwater still as he grasped for me, trying to calm me down. Another howl gushed from my throat, and then I was running.

A tree caught my shoulder, so I made sure the tree caught my fist.

Then I was running again.

My pulse was no longer a thrum but a steady gush in my ears. Tree limbs, dry and gnarled, whipped at my cheeks and the exposed flesh of my arms as I ran through the woods. Moments later, only the wind created by the propulsion of my body whipped at my skin as I ran. My eyes, unseeing, watered as I ran along the blacktop, putting distance between myself and…everything. I needed space. Wide open space. Everything was closing in around me. I didn't want trees or buildings or shack walls.

There was no air. I couldn't breathe. I couldn't hear. I couldn't stop running.

I would have run forever, my face meeting the sun as it rose each day, my feet refusing to stop. Potholes and careless feet, however, are a bad combination. The fiery blast of white-hot pain shot through my foot, up my ankle, and settled around my shin right before the palms of my hands and my knees met the rough blacktop.

The pain shooting up my leg kept me from immediately rising to my feet so I could dash off again. Sometimes, no matter how much a person wants to ignore it, we are defeated.

So, I flopped over, sitting down in the middle of the road. My injured leg lay out before me against the road. I didn't dare look at my ankle. The thrumming in my ears was gone and all I could hear was my ragged breath and the whistling of the warm summer breeze along the steaming asphalt.

"Wuh-hat are you duh-doing?" I didn't look up at the sound of Kevin's voice and his sneakers slapping against the road. *"Are you out of your—"*

Gasping for breath, I stared down at the knees of my jeans, torn and bloody. I held my hands out to find ragged flesh and blood oozing to the surface of the wounds. Kevin slid to a stop next to me, his words cutting off with one glance at my injuries. For the longest of moments, he stared down at me and I stared at my hands.

"Holy shit, Carson."

Kevin knelt down next to me, and his hand automatically reached for my ankle. At the first contact from his fingertips against my flesh, I winced. Kevin gasped.

"Oh, jeez." He pulled his hand back.

As my breathing calmed, and Kevin stared at my ankle, the thrumming in my ears returned. Not quite as loudly as before, it was still enough to block out the world around me. I was aware of Kevin standing, saying something, but I had no idea what he said. Then he disappeared from the corner of my vision.

When he returned, it could have been twenty minutes or twenty hours later. All I had done in that time was stare at the pools of blood forming in the palms of my hands. He said something, but I couldn't hear it. I didn't react. When he grabbed me under my armpits, my first instinct was to fight him. I wanted to stay in the road. Forever, preferably. I didn't have the energy to fight him, though.

Kevin put one of my arms over his shoulders and helped me hobble a few feet across the blacktop before he was nudging me into something large and metal.

The back of a pickup.

It took some work, but we finally got me up into the bed of the pickup. Kevin hopped into the back of the truck and closed the gate. Then he rapped his knuckles on the side of the bed and it took off as Kevin plopped down to sit across from me.

I had no idea whose pickup I was riding in, and I didn't care. Where they were taking me didn't matter.

The wind picked up and my hair danced in the golden twilight.

I still couldn't feel my injuries.

But I could hear the wind finally.

It sounded like Kevin's voice.

It was saying: *Why would you do this to yourself?*

Chapter 8

KEVIN

Carson's dad died on a Friday in the middle of August when the temperatures had soared so high that no one left their home unless necessary. They buried him on the following Tuesday under the shadow of a small white tent that was made to cover a gravesite and a few mourners, which was more than enough for the service. In the end, it was only Carson, his crutches, his aunt and uncle, Wallace Lee, me, and a few of the old-timers from town who showed up. The tent was plenty big to keep us all out of the torturous sun.

Carson stared down at his twisted ankle for the entire service, never once looking up. When it was over, his aunt Sara Lee Barton held a small reception at her home since Carson's place wasn't sufficient. I rode over with Wallace Lee since I had no car of my own.

Carson sat in the corner of his aunt's living room in an easy chair, his crutches stacked and leaning against the side of it. He stared down at nothing as the few of us mourners ate the offered food and gave our condolences to Mr. and Mrs. Barton. It was pitiful, the lack of mourners. The old-timers had only come for the gossip and to collect stories for their next meeting.

I would have felt bad for Carson if I felt that he was even aware that a funeral was going on. I hoped that he had saved some of the painkillers the hospital had given him for the day.

I'm not one for drugs or drinking, but I hoped Carson had the help in numbing himself to the day.

"*He's stayin' with us for now*," Sara Lee had murmured to Wallace Lee as the three of us stood by the food table, "*'til that ankle gets better. Says he wants to go home as soon as he can.*"

"*You think that's a good idea?*" Wallace Lee asked.

I stared out of the dining room into the living room at Carson. He was staring down at the floor, his expression blank.

"*It's the only thing he's said in days,*" Sara Lee said with a sigh. "*I reckon we should honor it.*"

Wallace Lee made a noise with his throat, as though agreeing, but cautiously.

After we'd been around long enough to be called polite, and we'd eaten the food Sara Lee had put out for the reception, Wallace Lee and I said our "goodbyes" and left. I'd tried to say something to Carson before leaving his aunt's house, but he didn't seem to realize I was even there. I settled for squeezing his shoulder, which he didn't seem to notice.

As Wallace Lee and I rode back home in his old pickup truck, with the air conditioner on full blast, we stayed silent. At least for the first part of our journey. There wasn't much that could be said for Carson and his loss. Death is inevitable, and Carson's father had been hiding from it for longer than anyone could have hoped. That didn't relieve any sorrow, however.

But there are hardly enough words for such a sorrow.

"He'll be fine," Wallace Lee said as we crossed the city limits back into town. "Out there by himself."

I turned to look at Wallace Lee, but he hadn't turned to look at me when he spoke. He was looking out at the road. Examining him for a moment, I realized he hadn't turned to look at me because he hadn't been speaking to me. He had been speaking to himself.

"Yeah," I said.

I wasn't speaking to Wallace Lee, either.

"I feel sorry for that boy," he said.

He still wasn't looking at me. However, a smile slowly came to Wallace Lee's mouth.

"I do feel sorry for that boy. I swear," he said, as though convincing himself.

I frowned at Wallace Lee and nearly asked him what he was smiling about. After the day we'd had—and the previous weeks, I let it go. I turned my head back to look out at the road rushing up to meet the truck.

Chapter 9

KEVIN

August surrendered itself to September and day after day, and even after Carson was brought back to his house to live by Sara Lee, he never came to the creek. His ankle had healed, so he had no excuse not to venture into the woods. Day after day, I'd go out to the woods after work, only to find that I was alone. The summer had come and gone, and the kids were back in school without so much as a drop of raining falling from the sky all season.

Sometimes, after my trips out to the woods, I'd sneak over to the tree line along Carson's property. I'd always find him sitting in the rocking chair on his porch. Each time he looked gaunter, more vacant. Instinct told me not to approach him because I wouldn't be welcome. However, I wanted to offer an ear or a shoulder if he wanted it.

But I kept my distance.

Wallace Lee had let it slip that Carson had asked him for a job when he found out his father was dying. He was simply waiting for Carson to let him know when he was ready to get to work. As was typical of Wallace Lee, he was being kind and giving Carson space to figure out when the time was right. He'd hold a job for Carson until then.

After over a week of not seeing Carson at the creek, I stopped going out into the woods every day. Instead, my walks home from work took me to Wallace Lee's house. I finally began taking him up on his offer of a beer each evening.

We'd sit and listen to the bees or watch the beekeepers when they showed up to water and feed the bees. Glad that the students from the college wore their beekeeping suits, I was amazed at how the bees swarmed them. Annoyed at having the students still trying to relocate them permanently, the bees showed their anger each time.

Wallace Lee and I did our best not to chuckle each time the swarms would startle the students, but the beers made it difficult.

Days went by and the temperature dropped slightly, though Texas was determined to have the hottest September in history. If not for the beers and the shade cast by the overhang of Wallace Lee's house, we would have melted each dusk that we sat out there and watched the bees.

One evening, as the sun was halfway past the horizon, and the last of the students was packing up to leave Wallace Lee's place, a funny thing happened. A single bee somehow managed to wiggle its way under the collar and inside the student's veil. Since it was a single bee, and the student quickly remedied the situation, Wallace Lee and I nearly pissed ourselves laughing at the squeals and screeches the student emitted while dealing with the bee.

Sheepishly, the student had waved at us as he hopped in his car and sped away, embarrassed at having freaked out over a single bee. The dust was barely settled in Wallace Lee's driveway before he turned to me in his chair. With a wink and a nod, he said:

"Bet that one doesn't come back."

I chuckled. "Nah. They all suh-seem duh-determined to save the bees. He'll be back."

"Might be right," Wallace Lee said, turning to lay back in his chair. "You know what I learned from them kids?"

He gestured vaguely towards the temporary hive.

"What?"

"Honey bees live about four weeks during summer. Up to six months in winter. And the average honey bee makes about a twelfth a teaspoon of honey in their life. They fly and pollinate and fly and pollinate some more, going like crazy to accomplish their life mission, and that mission is to make less honey than you put in a damned cup of tea."

I stared over at him with wide eyes.

"Seems like a waste of time to me," Wallace Lee said. "Watchu think?"

"I mean," I began, "if you like huh-honey, I guess it's a guh-good thing they're so dedicated. Right?"

He chuckled. "Sure enough. Insanity might be useful from time to time. If bees weren't crazy, we wouldn't have honey. Or crops. Or flowers. Maybe we should all go a little *bee crazy* from time to time?"

I laughed.

"Keep your eye on the mission, my boy," Wallace Lee tapped the arm of my chair with the bottom of his beer bottle. "Know that your life has meaning, even if it's hard to measure."

I nodded along as I sipped my beer.

That one sip drained what was left in my bottle. It was a good thing, as Wallace Lee and I had let time and common sense get away from us. We each had four empty bottles beside our chair legs. With a sigh, I stood and began to collect my empties.

"Nah," Wallace Lee waved me off. "Leave 'em. I'll take care of 'em."

"You sure?" I asked.

"Sure," he said with a nod up at me. "You headed home?"

I shrugged. "I guh-uess I should."

"Well, don't go stumblin' all over the road like a regular ole fool," he said with a grin. "I don't want to get no calls from the cops about some white boy stumblin' away from my house."

"I'm fuh-ine. I'm muh-more than fine."

"Sure, sure."

I laughed. "See?"

I took a few steady steps in a perfect line.

"Just enough buh-beer to feel guh-good but not enough to impair me," I said.

"All right," he said. "Be careful, though."

I gave him a mock salute, which made him chuckle. With another "thanks for the beers," I turned on my heels and headed out. As I walked through town, the beers in my belly put a lilt in my step. Before I knew what I was doing, my feet had carried me along the woods in the direction of Carson's house. The beers had made me feel jovial and invincible, as though if I showed up at my mourning friend's house, he'd be compelled to finally talk to me.

Maybe Carson wouldn't stare out at nothing for once. It was possible that, seeing me in such a good mood, he would be forced to say something. Anything. Even if he gave me a small smile, it would make things feel less horrible. The beer was enough to give me hope.

When I found myself emerging from the tree line onto Carson's lawn, his rocking chair on the porch was empty. The sun had ducked below the horizon and darkness was slowly creeping in, so I had to assume he had gone inside for the night. A single light shone through the window, but darkness continued to creep up on the house as the sun dipped further below the horizon.

Through the screen door, I could see that the front door was wide open. The lazy whirring of a fan that had seen better days sounded from inside. It was several seconds after my knuckles rapped on the weathered wooden frame of the screen door before Carson's face appeared. Haloed by the sickly yellow light cast by the lamp inside, the dark circles under his eyes and his gaunt face made Carson look like a corpse.

He stared blankly out at me, his eyes seeing nothing, and the beer in my belly no longer emboldened me. Carson said nothing, so we stared at each other through the screen for several seconds.

"I," I began slowly, "was juh-just cuh-oming to check on you."

Carson stared at me.

"Are—" I began, and then my eyes met Carson's.

He looked hollow, but also as if he was waiting on something. An event to set him back into motion—bring him back to life. The empty look in his eyes made him appear as though once he restarted, there was no guarantee that what he did would be good. In fact, something in those hollow eyes told me that he very much wanted a reason to do something not good. So that he could have his revenge on the world for bringing him such sorrow.

"—uh, yuh-you uh-okay? I duh-didn't nuh-know if yuh-you—"

I couldn't stop myself. My stutter wouldn't stop. When I start stuttering uncontrollably, it's not just my stutter that's the problem. It's the fact that I also can't stop speaking. So, not only am I stuttering, but my brain is also forcing bundles of words out of my mouth that would mean nothing even if someone could understand them. I could feel my face growing red as Carson stared at me as my mouth moved, though I could no longer hear what I was saying. I couldn't even hear in my head what it was I was trying to say.

When Carson pushed the screen door open, and I stepped back, stuttering and blathering, I knew what was coming. He was going to punch me. Knock me to my ass, if not clear off the porch. I'd retch up all of the beer in my belly on his front lawn, and he'd go back inside. No longer bothered by the incessant slop of words pouring from my mouth. But I couldn't make myself stop talking.

Carson stepped out onto the porch; the screen door slapping shut behind him. What came next wasn't his fist flying into my face. Instead, he stepped around me, and shuffled across the porch to his rocking chair. As he sat down, staring out blankly at the barren lawn, I somehow managed to stop talking. I found myself standing there, watching Carson as he sat motionless in the chair, staring at the yard that was as dead as his father.

Talking hadn't helped. I hadn't been able to do it without sounding ridiculous, anyway. So, I shuffled across the porch and sat down in the rickety old wooden chair next to Carson's rocking chair. And I stared out at the lawn with him.

In the moment, it occurred to me how mourning causes life to come to a standstill to the point that a person is hyperaware of everything around them. Things they hadn't given two thoughts to in the time leading up to a death are suddenly sharp and immediate. Carson's yard and the woods surrounding his property were deathly silent.

The cicadas hadn't sung all summer.

That's how bad our drought had been. Winged singing demons of heat couldn't even tolerate the conditions. The thought amused me, but I didn't dare smile. Instead, I turned my head to look at Carson. His chair was rocking ever so slightly, but his stare hadn't changed. His expression was still vacant.

Cautiously, I reached over and covered the hand he had on the arm of his chair with mine. He didn't respond, or even change expressions, but he didn't yank his hand away angrily, either.

"I'm suh-orry, Carson," I managed. "I'm ruh-really sorry."

He stared out at the lawn.

Through the night, we sat together on his front porch, unspeaking. Even as darkness enveloped the house and the light inside cast a single square of yellow gold on the dirt lawn, we sat. Uncertain of when it happened, I eventually fell asleep in the chair, still holding Carson's hand. I didn't wake until the sky was turning dark blue and blood red.

When I looked over, Carson was asleep in his chair, his head lolled to the side, away from me. I let go of his hand and rose from the chair quietly. Silently, I made my way off the porch and snuck away from his house. A half hour later, I returned with a couple of coffees in Styrofoam cups and lids and a bag of cheap breakfast sandwiches from the convenience store. It wasn't much, or even good, but it was fresh since the store had just opened for the day.

As I sat back down in the rickety wooden chair, the creaking roused Carson from his sleep. Lolling around like a water balloon on a stick, Carson's head rolled in my direction as his eyes fluttered open. He seemed surprised to see me still there—the only time his expression changed all night—but he quickly went back to looking hollow.

"I got coffee," I said softly. "And some breakfast."

Carson, true to form, said nothing, but he accepted the cup of coffee from me. He had flipped back the mouth guard and was taking a sip when I opened the bag of sandwiches. When I held one out to him, he didn't move to take it from me. I shoved it at him.

"Please," I said. "Puh-lease eat something, man."

Finally, he reached out and took the foil-wrapped sandwich from me, his fingers like twigs against mine as it slid from my hand to his. I unwrapped one of the sandwiches for myself and began to eat as the sun started to peek over the horizon beyond the trees. It took a few minutes, but Carson finally unwrapped his sandwich and began to nibble at it.

Within seconds he was devouring it as though it was the most delicious thing he'd ever tasted in his life. When he'd taken his last bite, I shoved another sandwich at him. He devoured it as well. I'd only bought four sandwiches, and I hadn't even finished one, but I shoved the last sandwich at him as well.

Once all of the sandwiches were gone, and we were left sitting there, staring at nothing, sipping our coffees, the sun was finally rising over the trees. I sat with Carson for as long as I could before I knew I couldn't waste any more time.

"I have to guh-go home and shuh-shower," I said quietly. "My shift at the stuh-store starts soon."

Carson said nothing, but he nodded ever so slightly. I rose from the chair and gathered up my cup and the empty bag and wrappers. I held the bag out for Carson to deposit his coffee cup. He did so without looking up at me.

"I'll come by after wuh-wuh-ork," I suggested. "To chuh...eck on you. I'll bring something to eat. O...kay?"

Though he remained silent, I caught the flick of his eyes in my direction. That was good enough for me. I made my way down the front steps, the crumbled bag full of trash gripped in my fist. I turned to look up at Carson.

"Sleep," I said. "You puh-robably need it."

Then I turned and walked away. I hadn't even made it to the tree line before the sound of Carson's screen door slapping shut reached my ears.

Chapter 10

CARSON

We were walking through the woods. As we had been doing each day for a week. I led the way silently, my feet crunching through the detritus. Summer was going for one last hurrah. The heat was overwhelming, the sun scorching, and if we'd had any rain to speak of recently, it would have been humid enough to snatch our breath away. Instead, we were left with the dry, crackly air that seemed to bake my lungs with each breath I took.

Kevin walked behind me, giving me enough distance to be comfortable, but close enough so that I wouldn't forget he was there. I wanted to hate him for the kindness he'd shown me day after day. I wanted to think of it as pity. He was being a friend, though. Kevin was doing the only thing he knew how to do—especially since I couldn't force myself to say anything—he was staying present.

If he wasn't covering a shift at the convenience store, he was at my house or following me through the woods. A day didn't go by that every spare second he had in his life wasn't devoted to making sure I knew he was there. When I was ready.

We both knew that going out to the creek once again would be pointless, but we had begun doing it every day regardless.

As it had been for months on end, when we arrived at the clearing that cut through the woods, we were greeted by the dry, dusty gulch that slashed its way through the land. Kevin came to stand beside me as we stared down at the empty crevice.

Finally, after what seemed like forever, Kevin broke the silence.

"Look," he said excitedly, nudging his hand against my forearm.

I looked over at him to find him staring up at the sky. Tilting my head back, I looked up at the sky. A wisp of cotton was floating by lazily. It was barely a cloud, just enough to qualify, though the blue sky beyond peeked through it. When I looked over at Kevin, he was looking at me and smiling.

"Maybe tomorrow?" he asked.

I nodded and looked back up at the sky.

Over the next few days, as September grew on us, the heat subsided enough to make it clear that summer was on its way out. It was still too hot for the month, but it was a relief from the previous months' temperatures.

Each day, Kevin and I made our way out to the woods. I could tell, as the days went by, that he was growing frustrated with me. I hadn't uttered a word to him since before my dad had died. Something inside of me had stolen my voice. It wasn't that I didn't want to speak. That I didn't want to tell everyone who cared even a little bit how I felt. I wanted to scream and howl and slam my fists into the trees until either the tree gave up or the skin on my knuckles split until bone was showing and blood dripped down my forearms to give life to the dead earth.

I simply couldn't. I didn't have the strength or energy.

Then again, I was worried that if I started to talk—*especially, if I started to punch things*—that I would never stop.

So, I led Kevin through the woods each day silently, to the creek and back. To the creek and back. Our feet crunching on dead leaves and twigs and the dry, crackly air scorching our lungs. Every now and then, Kevin would say something. Mention a wisp of a cloud in the sky. How he thought cooler weather was finally going to settle in for good. Sometimes I'd nod. Sometimes I wouldn't respond at all, simply because I couldn't figure out how to respond.

But I knew that even if I couldn't talk, I wanted Kevin there to not talk to. Having him by my side as I marched through the woods made going home to an empty house each night easier. I began to realize that the hours between seeing Kevin after his shift at the convenience store and him showing up at the house to walk through the woods with me were the longest hours of my day. The time we spent walking through the woods together, though I said nothing, seemed to fly by.

As I'd feared, after another week went by, it was obvious that Kevin was getting frustrated with me. Annoyed at being ignored each time he said something. It was on a Friday, when we were standing at the creek, and a merciful breeze was whistling through the clearing, that he turned to stare at me. I could feel his eyes boring into the side of my head.

"Say something."

I glanced at him out of the corner of my eye.

"*Anything*," he pleaded. "Say suh-something, Carson."

My brain wanted to respond, but the tugging in my chest caught the words in my throat.

"Fine," Kevin sighed and turned back to the creek. "Fuh-ine."

Seconds ticked by as I did my best to figure out how to be a person again. But the words wouldn't come. Finally, Kevin turned away from the creek and began to walk back towards the woods. I wanted to shout at him to not leave me out there by myself. To stay. But all I could do was turn and watch him as he walked towards the trees. I didn't want to see him slip away into the woods, but I couldn't figure out how to speak up.

At the tree line, Kevin saved me from myself. He spun on his heels and glared at me, his face red with annoyance.

"You can't suh-say anything?" he barked. "Not one word?"

I couldn't.

"Muh-man," he sighed, throwing his hands up lazily, "I can't just fuh-follow you around like an idiot, wuh-waiting for you to act human, Carson. This silence is kuh-illing me. You've got to suh-say something. *Something*. Anything. Just...*fucking talk*."

Frustrated with whatever it was inside of me keeping my voice suppressed, I decided to give up. I turned and walked towards the woods as well. I could go home and be silent. Where no one would be mad at me if I had nothing to say. As I walked past Kevin, he reached out and his fingers latched around my forearm. Stopping, I shot an angry look down at his hand.

"*Fucking talk to me, Carson!*" he barked.

I tried ripping my arm out of his grasp, but he held tight.

"Tuh-talk to me, damnit!"

I jerked my arm again, but Kevin's fingers dug into my flesh.

"*Not tuh-talking won't bring your duh-dad back, goddamnit!*"

The next thing I knew, Kevin was staring at me with wide eyes. My forearm was across his neck, and I was pinning him against the tree he'd been standing by. I'd shoved my face in his, glowering at him, so close that I knew he would be able to feel my breath. If there was ever a time I could speak, that surely would have been it. But the words still wouldn't come. I settled for showing all of my rage and frustration on my face as I pinned him to the tree.

"*Carson*," Kevin whispered, his voice hoarse from my arm digging into his throat.

Something about the way he said my name brought me back to my senses and jolted my brain into thinking rationally once again. Slowly, I slid my forearm from Kevin's throat and fought to chase the glower from my face. Kevin stared at me with those wide eyes as my arm slid away from his throat and I inched back from his face. As soon as my arm was clear and I had put a few inches between our chests, Kevin growled and shoved me.

I stumbled, but just barely, widening the space between us.

"*Fuck you!*" Kevin barked.

There was a pink mark across Kevin's throat where my forearm had rested. I hadn't been aware how roughly I'd been pinning him to the tree.

He shoved me again.

"*Fuh-fucking psycho!*"

Once more he shoved me. Grunting from the force, I refused to stumble again.

"Wuh-what is *actually* ruh-wrong with you, man?" Kevin growled. "Are you fucking crazy?"

When Kevin pushed out with his arms to shove me again, something inside of me flipped. As his hands connected with my chest, I grabbed his wrists and pushed back. Forcing his arms back towards him, I pinned Kevin to the tree with my body, but I didn't shove my arm into his throat again. Kevin gasped as I stared blankly into his face, pinning his arms between our bodies.

Shuddering, Kevin breathed out raggedly as we stared into each other's eyes. A bead of sweat dribbled down his temple and over his cheek as the seconds ticked by and our eyes stayed locked. Kevin's breath felt hot against my face, and I knew that

I was returning the sensation to him. I slowly let my fingers loosen around his wrists, but I didn't move to unpin his arms from between us.

Raggedly, I breathed in and out, trying to control myself as Kevin stared at me, his expression changing from frightened to curious. That look forced me to move back, not much, but enough to free his arms from being trapped between us. Slowly, his arms slid down between us, from between our chest, grazing our stomachs, to our waists.

I wanted to be surprised—*or furious*—when Kevin's fingers trailed along the edge of my waistband. For some reason, I continued to stare into his eyes, my expression no longer rageful and angry. Instinctively, a hand shot up and I grabbed Kevin's wrist. He froze and stared back at me as I gripped his wrist. His fingers were still against my waistband, and I made no effort to remove them.

After what seemed like an eternity, I was shocked to find that I wasn't pulling Kevin's hand away, but slowly pushing it lower. I was as surprised as Kevin was when I laid his hand against me and found that I was excited. More excited than I'd been in years. When I removed my hand from Kevin's wrist, his hand cupped me, not pulling away. My arms went up and my hands went to the tree behind him, bracing myself; trapping Kevin between the tree and me.

He could have slipped away. There was enough room for him to maneuver and duck under my arms. But he didn't. His hand began to move against me. Gently at first, testing how I felt under his hand, through the fabric of my jeans. A sharp breath was forced from my lungs as I continued to stare into his eyes.

Kevin drew a soft moan from me as his hand firmly, yet gently, slid up and down the front of my jeans, feeling all of me through my jeans. I shuddered involuntarily but refused to close my eyes. I didn't want to stop looking onto his.

He spoke one more time. He said my name. Softly.

Then his hand went back up to my waistband and slid inside. There wasn't nearly enough room for Kevin's hand and what he found inside, but he somehow wrapped his fingers around me. Another moan escaped my throat as I stared into his eyes and his hands slid up and down the length of me. My hands clutched at the tree, and I continued to moan as Kevin's arm moved up and down, his hand continuing to stroke me.

When Kevin suddenly pulled his hand out of my pants, slick and shiny, I wanted to beg him to put his hand back where it had been. The hungry look in his eyes as he looked down and both of his hands went to the waist of my jeans once again stopped the words from my leaving my mouth. Moments later, he had undone my pants and shoved my jeans and underwear down to mid-thigh.

There wasn't enough distance between us, so I was poking against the front of his jeans, leaving a wet mark at his groin. Kevin stared down at me for moment, his eyes ablaze with an emotion I'd never seen in him before, and then he was tearing at the front of his pants.

He didn't shove them down like he'd done to me. He pushed his jeans and underwear down and somehow pried his feet, shoes and all, out of them. I looked down between us to find that the two of us were poking against each other. As soon as he was out of his pants, I moved forward excitedly and pinned Kevin against the tree with the length of my body.

It was his turn to moan as I trapped both of us between our bellies and swiveled my hips, rubbing us together. My hand came up to grip his jaw, forcing him to look into my eyes as I thrust against him slowly. Grunting with pleasure, I began to speed up, thrusting my length along his length, our bellies pressing us together.

When Kevin wrapped his arms around my neck, I found myself lifting him so he could wrap his legs around my waist. I pushed against him, pressing his back against the ragged bark of the tree as I reached under Kevin. My hand grabbed what it was searching for, and I guided it to Kevin. When I made contact, my eyes went to his.

Finding nothing but desire and desperation staring back at me, I continued my motions. Minutes later, I was fully inside of Kevin, thrusting rhythmically as he kept his arms wrapped around my neck, moaning with each thrust. I had one hand braced against the tree and another between us, stroking him as I moved in and out of him.

Sweat dripped from us and our hair was plastered to our skulls within minutes. It didn't stop us. I'm unsure how long we were there, against the tree, him in my hand, and me inside of him, but it never could have lasted long enough.

When it was over, and my hand and the fronts of our shirts were splattered, and I was spent, still inside of Kevin, we were gasping for breath. We stayed like that for a minute, Kevin pinned against the tree with his legs and arms around me, with me still inside of him. I'm not sure who made the first move, but finally, Kevin's arms and legs slid from around me and I slid out of him. Then we were standing too close to each other by the tree once again.

Wordlessly, I pulled my pants up as Kevin wiggled back into his. As he was zipping up and fastening the button, Kevin glanced at me. His cheeks were red, but I wasn't certain if it was from embarrassment or the heat. His hair was plastered to his forehead.

"I'm guh-going to guh-go huh-home now," he said.

"Don't leave," I exhaled the words.

Then he slipped away into the woods. And I fell forward, bracing myself against the tree.

Chapter 11

KEVIN

"This place is a money pit," Ralph said casually. "Don't know why I ever bought this godforsaken store to begin with."

I handed the change over to the customer I had been checking out—Mrs. Freelance, a local English teacher—and said "goodbye" to her. Once she was out the door, I turned to my boss with a curious look. He was staring up at the ceiling by the soda coolers, an annoyed frown on his face.

"What?" I asked.

"We just had to replace that damned air conditioner," he said as the bell over the door chimed, "and now we got cracks in the ceiling. This summer has killed us. All this dryness has caused the ground to shift and it's tryin' to tear this damned building down."

I started to speak, but Wallace Lee's voice stopped me.

"You want to sell out, you just let me know, Ralph," he said with a chuckle.

I turned to find him approaching the register as he dug his wallet out of his back pocket.

"I don't mind adding businesses to my portfolio," Wallace Lee quipped.

He looked up at me and winked. I smiled back and automatically reached for the packs of Marlboro Reds.

"I ain't sellin' to you!" Ralph exclaimed, though he sounded amused. "You'd have a damn monopoly in this town!"

Wallace Lee chuckled again and passed me a ten. I rang him up and passed him change. He winked at me once more and headed for the door. He never stayed to chat when anyone else was in the store. Though time had passed, and supposedly times were changing in town, Wallace Lee never let other people in town see how well the two of us got along. It hurt my heart, but I didn't stop him from doing what he thought was best.

"Well," he said as he reached for the doorhandle, "if you decide to do what's the right thing, you just holler!"

Ralph chuckled, but I couldn't tell if he was being polite, or he actually found it funny. Once Wallace Lee was out of the store, I began wiping down the counter and cleaning up around the register. With only fifteen minutes left in my shift, I needed to get things ready for Danielle.

"I guess I'll have to start doin' some patches around here," Ralph mumbled to himself. "No sense in payin' someone else to come in and do it. Just a waste of money. A pit."

I smiled and continued to clean. Having Ralph around the store for a few days, mumbling angrily to himself as he fixed up the store was not ideal. However, his running commentary, and annoyance, was comical. When Danielle arrived, she noticed Ralph muttering in the corner immediately. We exchanged amused glances, and I whispered a short synopsis of the day's events. Rolling her eyes, she ushered me out the door.

Cooler than it had been in months, it was almost pleasant outside. Still warm, but not as suffocatingly hot as it had been for months. When I'd arrived at work that morning, I promised myself that after work I would walk straight home. There was no point stopping at Wallace Lee's house since I knew it was inventory day at the grocery store and he'd be there until the late hours of the night.

And I wouldn't go to Carson's. I wouldn't go anywhere near his house.

I'd go home.

But my feet decided the day for me. I didn't go to Wallace Lee's, and I didn't go to Carson's. My feet directed me to the woods. Walking through the woods kept me from breaking my promise to not go to Carson's, but it allowed fate to decide where the day would take me.

My mind was garbled with the previous day's events. I could still physically recall what Carson and I had done. Somehow, I still felt full, as if there was a pressure in my lower parts. I knew it wasn't true, but my mind made me feel that it was true.

As I walked through the woods, my gut was fluttering, and against my will, I was slowly becoming excited. Between the ghostly full feeling and my excitement becoming more evident with each step, I was nearly walking bowlegged when I arrived at the creek. And fate spoke up.

It had been obvious that Carson would be at the creek when I arrived. I knew that when I had set out from the store. I had only told myself that I was leaving things up to fate so that I wouldn't feel embarrassed by my excitement at the possibility of finding him there.

Carson's head turned as I stepped up to the creek beside him. For a few seconds, I refused to look at him, but he didn't avert his gazed. When I finally turned my head to look at him, his expression was guarded, yet quizzical.

"I'm not guh-gay," I said.

The space of a breath passed.

"I'm not either," he said.

"I duh-don't even think I'm buh-bisuh-sexual or anything," I said.

He nodded. "Me either."

I nodded back and we turned to look down at the empty creek.

"Do you want to do it again?" Carson asked. "Now?"

"Yes."

"Here?" he asked, still looking down at the creek. "Or we can go to my house."

I looked up and around at the brown, dead woods around us.

"Luh-let's go to your house," I said.

Silently, we turned in unison and began our march out of the woods. But neither of us led and neither of us followed. We walked alongside each other silently, the crackling under our feet the soundtrack for our travels. My excitement didn't abate the whole way to Carson's house. I was nearly crazed with it when we walked up the steps and slipped inside his house. Carson closed the door behind us once we were inside, the darkness of his house enveloping us.

What happened next wasn't the angry desperation from the day before, though the obvious nervous excitement we both felt was apparent. Our fingers shook and twitched as we pulled our shirts off of each other and undid each other's pants. But I didn't throw my arms around Carson's neck and my legs around his waist as he pushed me up against a wall or threw me to the floor.

The next few moments found Carson's lips and tongue exploring my neck and chest. My stomach. Lower places. My moans filled the room as he spent what felt like an eternity that I never wanted to end exploring my body. After he rose and I did the same to him, we made our way to his bed and gently lowered ourselves to it.

Carson's thrusts were gentler, kinder, as he braced himself above me with my legs hooked over his shoulders. His moans joined mine and we created a symphony of pleasure that echoed from every corner of his house. Silent tears slipped from Carson's eyes and fell noiselessly to my chest. Using my thumbs, I wiped his eyes clear as he continued to thrust rhythmically into me.

I'm sorry. He had whispered that phrase to me numerous times. And I knew he wasn't talking about our current activities.

When he was done and spent, he slid down my body and greedily coaxed the same explosion from me. His sweat-damp hair was twined between my fingers as I stared up at his ceiling and stars exploded in my vision.

Then we lay in his bed and waited for the energy to repeat our activities.

When darkness filled the windows and it was apparent the day was done, the two of us fell asleep in his bed. Not quite holding each other, but not quite not holding each other, Carson was on his back with one of my arms and one of my legs draped over his naked body as we drifted off to sleep.

As my eyes shut lazily and my mind gave itself over to sleep, I wondered what we were doing. And why. What did it mean? Did what we'd done change who I was? Who was Carson? Why was I letting someone who had caused me such grief in our childhood do these things to me?

My final thought, as my eyes slid shut, was that I never wanted that full feeling in my lower parts to go away.

Chapter 12

CARSON

We were lying in the grass inside the tree line by the creek, the blades like steel wool against my shoulder blades. My arms were over my head, my hands folded under my head as a makeshift pillow. Kevin was lying on his side, his head propped up by one hand as his finger slowly traced its way from my bellybutton towards my chest. I was grinning, but my eyes were shut as I used my other senses to enjoy the touch against my flesh.

Kevin chuckled when I shivered and he pulled his hand away.

"Don't stop," I whispered.

Naked as jay birds in the woods, the warm breeze of the mid-September day against our skin, and Kevin exploring my body with his fingers, made me feel light. Free.

"O-okay."

The fingertip returned to my chest, and he traced up between my pecs slowly. Along my collarbones, and down one side, making me shiver again. We both laughed, but his finger continued its circuitous journey around my torso.

"Do you think it's different for us?" Kevin asked softly.

He hadn't explained what he meant, but I understood his meaning immediately. The serious change in conversation didn't chase the grin from my face, but I took the question seriously.

"I don't know."

He didn't say anything, but his finger continued its journey.

"Do you?" I asked.

"Why are we doing this?" he asked.

"You know why," I said.

"Yeah," he said. "It fuh-feels good. Buh-but luh-lots of things feel good."

I knew what he meant because I had been avoiding my true thoughts when I had answered his question. The obvious reason for our recent actions was not the real reason. I sighed, my eyes still closed, and took his hand in mine. I pressed it flat against my chest so that every inch of skin of his hand touched a part of my chest. I slid my hand from his.

"I'm r...eally not guh-gay," Kevin murmured.

His tone would have made any person believe he was lying to himself. However, I believed him. Because I wasn't gay either.

"I believe you," I said.

"I'm ruh-really not."

"And I really believe you."

"Then," he said, "wuh-why duh-do we duh-do this?"

I paused for a moment before letting one of my eyes crack open to look up at him. The sunlight that managed to sneak between the tree limbs above shone down and danced around his head, haloing him in light. For a second, I didn't see Kevin. I only saw someone who was touching me intimately. Comforting me. Pleasuring me.

"Do I make you nervous?"

Kevin swallowed hard, but his hand stayed on my chest.

"You've been stuttering a lot more."

"Yes," Kevin answered immediately, yet quietly.

"Don't be nervous."

"I cuh-can't help it."

I laid my hand over his again and opened my other eye to look up at him.

"We shuh-shouldn't do be doing this."

"Why?" I asked. "Do you want to stop?"

"No."

Using my hand to drag his up and over my chest, I stared up into Kevin's eyes and he stared back. Slowly, I dragged his hand over my chest, up to my neck, to my mouth. I kissed the palm of his hand as Kevin stared into my eyes, breathing raggedly. I took the very tip of his index finger in my mouth, sucking on it briefly. Then I bit down on it ever so slightly, not enough to hurt, but enough to make it obvious I was biting him.

Kevin laughed and yanked his hand away.

"Jerk," he said.

I chuckled and sighed happily as I stretched in the grass.

"I've nuh-never really been naked in fuh-ront of other people," Kevin said. "And you've seen me naked a muh-million times."

"It's only been a few days," I said.

He shrugged, looked off towards the creek on the other side of the tree line.

"I like doing this," I said, surprising myself.

Kevin didn't respond. He eyes stayed fixed on the creek.

"I don't know why," I said, though I knew why. I didn't want to say it out loud. "But I do. If you like it, too, we should keep doing it as long as we want. We can do whatever we want, Kevin."

It was the longest sentence I'd said in weeks. Sex does that to a guy, regardless of who is providing the sex.

Kevin mumbled something I couldn't quite hear.

"What?"

"Like the bees," Kevin said.

"What?" I laughed.

Sighing, he turned to me, and the smile on his face was genuine.

"Like the bees," he repeated. "Wallace Lee has buh-bees."

"Like," I frowned, "actual bees?"

Kevin nodded. "Students from the university buh-built a muh-makeshift hive on his property. Because of the duh-rought. They're trying to save them. Buh-but the bees are buh-being difficult."

I had no idea what the bees had to do with us.

"Wallace Lee suh-aid that bees don't luh-like being told what to do," Kevin said with a shrug. "I guess we're luh-like the bees. We do what we want."

We stared at each other for what felt like forever. I wanted to grab Kevin and repeat the thing we had finished doing a half hour before, but I also wanted Kevin to keep talking.

"Why won't the bees do what they want?" I asked.

Kevin's shoulders rose and fell again. "They think they duh-don't want to abandon their old huh-hive. It might have huh...oney in it or something."

Slowly, I sat up, a grin blooming on my face. Kevin returned my grin with a quizzical look.

"You know what that sounds like to me?" I asked, reaching for my pants.

Putting on my pants wasn't what I really wanted to do, because that meant we were done with our current activity. However, we could do that again whenever we wanted.

"Wuh-what?" Kevin asked.

"Free honey," I said as I slipped a leg into my jeans.

Chapter 13

KEVIN

We heard the buzzing from the makeshift hive at the edge of Wallace Lee's property before we saw it. Having walked from the creek in silence, the buzzing was a welcome sound. The entire walk I'd wanted to talk to Carson about...everything. I wanted to ask him to say out loud the one thing we both weren't saying. I wanted to ask him why he was *this* when he had been *that* in high school. I wanted to know why he had been *that* in high school.

I wanted to talk about boundaries. When was it okay to do what we were doing? *Where* was it okay? How often were we going to do it? Was it okay that I wanted to do it often? How long did he think it would last? How did it make him feel?

What did it mean to each of us?

Did it change who we were?

"Do you think they're making more honey in that new hive?" Carson's asked as we stood a few yards within the tree line.

The makeshift hive and the mobile garden could be seen around the skeletal trees on Wallace Lee's property. Little black dots floated and whizzed around the hive that looked like a white chest of drawers on long legs. Or maybe a stack of storage containers with lids atop legs. It was an odd, unappealing looking decoration in the yard.

"Huh?"

"You said that Wallace Lee said the bees were being difficult?" Carson glanced at me, then went back to staring through the woods at the hive. "Are they refusing to make honey here?"

"I don't know."

"If they are," Carson said, though I'm not sure he was actually talking to me, "it might be because their old hive is full, and they want to get back to it."

"Muh-aybe?" I responded. "He said that the buh-bees kept tuh-rying to get back to their old hive."

Carson was grinning. "Honey."

"They huh-have honey at the stuh-store," I chuckled nervously.

Carson turned to me, the tree casting a shadow across his face like a slash as he held up the glass jar he'd run into his house to grab.

"But this honey is free."

"I don't want to do anything stuh-stupid," I said.

I wanted to do something stupid.

I desperately wanted to do something stupid.

"We won't do anything stupid," Carson said, and I could tell even he didn't believe it. "We're just going to get some honey that's up for grabs. That's all."

I wasn't sure what to say to Carson, or if there was anything to say at all. However, I was concerned with how he thought we were going to get honey out of the hive. I'd seen the bees swarm the college students when they came to tend to the bees, and they'd worn protective clothing to keep from being stung. Carson and I had nothing to protect us from being stung to death. If we approached the hive, we were basically wishing for death. No honey was worth that, no matter how much I loved it.

"They'll swuh-warm us if we tuh-try to get to the hive," I whispered.

Carson continued to stare at the makeshift hive.

"If we guh-go over there—"

He turned to me, looking at me as though I was the craziest person he'd ever met.

"Not *that* hive," he said. "We don't even know if they've made honey in there. They probably have started," he explained, "but I'm talking about the honey in their old hive."

My brow furrowed with confusion.

"They were taken from that hive and moved here, right?"

I nodded.

"That means that their old hive is probably full of honeycomb—and honey," Carson said. "If we can find it, it's all ours. The bees are *here*. The honey is *there*. We can just walk right up and take it."

Elated that we weren't going to try to get into the makeshift hive, I still had many questions.

"How wuh-will we find the old huh-hive?"

"You said that Wallace Lee said that the college students said—"

I laughed and Carson stopped to chuckle for a second.

"—that the bees keep trying to get back to their old hive, right?"

Nodding, I swallowed down my fear.

"If we watch, we'll see where some of them go to in the woods, right?" he asked. "If a few of them are zipping away to check on the old hive, we just follow them and they'll lead us to the old hive. Then we can get the honey."

"Thuh-that means there'll be buh-ees there."

"Just a few," he said with a shrug. "A few bees are easy to deal with."

"You're guh-etting the honey," I nudged him with my elbow.

"Deal."

So, the two of us watched the bees buzzing around the makeshift hive just beyond the trees. Waiting for a sign that some of them were going to zip through the woods to their old hive. Most of the bees stayed swarming around, buzzing angrily, as though they'd never accept the stacked white boxes on legs as their home. But they didn't seem to be flying far from the hive, either.

For the longest time, it seemed as though the bees were going to be difficult with us as well. Their angry buzzing around the hive wasn't doing anything to lead us to their old home. Time and time again, bees would zip from the hive towards the woods, filling us with anxious hope, only to flit back towards the makeshift hive. After a while, I began to suspect that Carson might give up.

I hoped that he would.

The longer we waited, the more nervous I became. I didn't dare speak, knowing every single word from my mouth would be a stutter. The buzzing, now filling my ears and clouding my thoughts, seemed to be whispering "danger" each time. I wanted to go along with Carson's plan—something inside of me was compelling me to do anything he wanted—but I was nervous.

Finally, as I began to feel Carson's excitement for the honey slipping away, a handful of bees—maybe a dozen—zipped away from the hive and into the woods. Carson's face lit up and his head whipped around to look at me. With a grin, he bolted away, chasing after the bees. Reluctantly, I took off in a jog after him.

Racing through the woods, paying attention to Carson, and not the sound of the bees, I did my best to keep pace. I hoped that he was paying attention to where the bees were going, though I had no idea how we could possibly track such small creatures through the woods. Of course, with all of the trees skeletal from the relentless summer, it was easier to spot the bees as they flew away.

Uncertain if it was my nerves that skewed time or not, we seemed to run forever through the woods, chasing after the bees. However, it couldn't have possibly been more than a few minutes. When Carson stopped, maybe a half mile from Wallace Lee's place, holding his arm out to slow me down, I skidded to a stop beside him.

With one arm across my chest, he pointed to his ear with his other hand as we stood there, catching our breaths in the middle of the woods. As my blood stopped thumping in my ears, it was replaced with the sound of buzzing. Not the sound of buzzes drifting away as the bees flew, but nearby. As though they had stopped.

Carson grinned at me and jerked his head towards the woods ahead. Turning to check out what he'd seen, I found that we had stopped a few yards away from an old dead tree. Cleaved off halfway down its trunk by…God knew what…I could see a few bees buzzing around the top. Apparently hollowed out, the top of the trunk allowed the bees access to the inside of the tree.

The old hive had to be in the tree trunk.

"*Honey,*" Carson whispered to me.

I nodded slowly, my gut twisting in knots, as I stared at the bees flitting around the opening to the tree.

"*Thuh-they'll sting you,*" I said.

"*There aren't that many,*" Carson whispered back. "*I can take a few stings if they get feisty.*"

"*You're cub-razy.*"

"*Maybe.*"

He chuckled. The idea of doing something so dangerous making him laugh caused me to frown. Was he really going to walk up to the tree—assuming the bees wouldn't sting him immediately upon seeing him—stick his hand blindly into the tree, and grope around for honeycomb? Even if Carson made it up to the tree without getting stung, there was no way he wouldn't get stung once he reached into the tree.

Was anything worth that risk?

"*Okay,*" Carson said resolutely, "*wish me luck.*"

He began to creep forward. I grabbed a handful of the back of his shirt.

"*Don't,*" I whisper-hissed.

He turned his head to look over his shoulder.

"*It'll be fine,*" he assured me. "*I'll grab some honeycomb, slip it into the jar, and we'll run away. No big deal, man.*"

The lump in my throat was advising me to hold onto Carson's shirt, to refuse to let him go through with his plan. However, when he began creeping away once again, his shirt slipped from my grip. I was forced to watch him tiptoe through the woods towards the tree.

As quietly as he could, Carson crept towards the old, dead tree and the buzzing of the angry, displaced bees. I tried to convince myself that the handful of bees buzzing around the top of the tree couldn't do enough damage if Carson angered them. Even if every single bee stung him, he'd be fine. There would be pain, surely, but it would be more inconvenient than dangerous.

Time seemed to slow, then stop, as Carson made his way to the tree quietly. Somehow, the buzzing of the bees seemed to get louder and fill my ears as Carson stepped up to the tree. Beside the trunk, he paused and turned his head to look at me over his shoulder. He gave me a reassuring smile, which I tried to return without looking nervous.

Finally, he turned back to the tree and his hand slowly rose towards the top of the tree. My breath was like a rock in my throat as I watched his hand crest the top of the tree and slowly dive into the hollowed trunk below. The bees swarmed around the top of the tree, a few zipped around Carson's head, but he had so far avoided getting stung.

As his hand slid into the trunk and out of view, Carson's body went rigid. And the buzzing seemed to fill the woods around us. Unable to breathe, I stared in horror as Carson's head turned towards me. He was no longer smiling. His face was ashen.

"*RUN!*" he screamed.

The jar fell from his hand, shattering at the base of the tree.

Chapter 14

KEVIN

"You get into some poison ivy?" I jerked at the sound of Wallace Lee's voice.

I'd barely wrapped my fingers around the bottle of calamine lotion on the shelf when his question had stopped me. Slipping the bottle from the shelf, I turned to find Wallace Lee standing next to me, a clipboard in his hand. I hadn't wanted to go to the Sav-A-Ton for the lotion, but our options were limited. Carson had zero medical supplies in his house, and I knew that we didn't have any calamine at my house. The convenience store didn't sell medical supplies, so that left the Sav-A-Ton.

"Nuh-no," I said. "Uh, bee sting."

Wallace Lee's brow furrowed as he looked me over.

"Where'd they get ya'?" he asked.

"Carson," I mumbled. "He guh-got stung."

He shook his head.

"You boys been out there messin' with them bees?" It was supposed to be an admonishment, but there was an undertone of amusement to his question.

The red that was creeping up my cheeks told him all he needed to know. Wallace Lee "tsked" and shook his head again. He started to turn and walk away, but with a concerned shake of his head, he met my eyes once more.

"You boys don't be getting' in any trouble out there you can't get yourselves out of," he said sternly.

"We wuh-wuh-won't," I said.

With a fiery, fatherly look in his eyes, Wallace Lee gave me a nod, then turned and walked away.

I hustled to the front of the store and checked out as quickly as I could, not wanting to have to look into Wallace Lee's eyes again. Something in the way he looked at me told me that he was concerned about the time I was spending with Carson. Or maybe he was simply upset that we'd obviously done something stupid enough to get Carson stung by bees. The fact was, I *knew* Wallace Lee felt something was going on with Carson and me.

There was no way he'd know, but I knew it.

It could have been my own fear of anyone finding out, but I couldn't shake the feeling as I walked from the Sav-A-Ton back out to the woods. Wallace Lee always saw and heard more than he ever let on. The rest of the people in town tended to be up their own asses too much to ever really know the facts about anything. But not Wallace Lee. He paid attention.

Carson was still sitting along the bank of the dry creek when I got back out to the woods. The welts on his face and arms were no worse than they'd been when I'd left to go to the Sav-A-Ton, but they were no better. He was wincing and squeezing the last stinger out of a welt on his forearm when I sat down next to him.

"Eleven," he said, sighing.

He didn't look over at me. He was still examining the welts on his arms and running his fingertips across the ones on his face.

"You're lucky," I said, pulling the lotion from the bag.

"I guess."

"You cuh-ould of died."

"Yeah."

"Is thuh-that all yuh-you're going to say?"

Carson chuckled as his cheeks reddened. Shaking my head, as though scolding a puppy who had piddled on the floor, I vigorously shook the bottle of pink lotion. He watched as I peeled the plastic protective wrapping from around the cap, unscrewed the cap, removed the little sticker that covered the opening, then returned the cap to the bottle. When I flipped the lid, he held his hand out.

"I can do it," he said.

"You cuh-an't see the stings on yuh-your fuh-ace."

He lowered his arm and didn't fight me.

Using my fingertip, since I didn't have any cotton balls or a rag, I squeezed a healthy dollop of the lotion out and reached for Carson's face. He turned his head so that I could easily get to the four stings on his cheeks and forehead, but he didn't look up at me. Meticulously, making sure to cover the welts thoroughly, I applied the lotion to Carson's face.

"Why are you being nice to me?" he asked, his voice barely a whisper.

"It's easier fuh-for me to—"

"Not now," he said, cutting me off. "At all. Why are you being nice to me?"

I sighed.

"Ian asked muh-me to wuh-watch over you."

He nodded slowly. "To pity me."

I jabbed my fingertip into one of Carson's welts and he winced, but he didn't pull away or scream at me.

"I duh-don't puh-pity you," I said firmly.

"But you wouldn't be nice to me if Ian hadn't asked?"

"I'd stuh-ill me nice t...o you."

"The...stuff we do," Carson asked slowly, "do you do that because you want to? Or because you think Ian would want you to? I don't want you to feel like—"

"Ian and Muh-mike cuh-an't make a guh-uy do gay things."

"I know that. That's not what I meant."

"I duh-don't know wuh-why. I juh-ust want to."

He nodded again. "I want to, too. And I don't know why. But it's just sex. I'm not gay."

That made perfect sense to me.

"Yeah," I said.

"Nothing more."

"Yeah."

"Okay."

Carson didn't have to explain his intentions in speaking about the sexual relationship we'd developed. He was confirming that we had sex and it was about having sex. No more; no less. No one was going to be hurt when it ended. Neither of us expected anything more, nor did we want it. And neither of us could precisely explain why we did it, though we knew why we were doing it. It made no sense, but at least we were in agreement.

"I'm glad my dad's dead," Carson said suddenly, but his voice was a whisper.

I paused only for a moment before dabbing at another welt on his upper arm. There was really nothing I could say to that, so I waited for him to continue his thought. If he wanted.

"And I'm sad," he said.

I understood that, too.

"He used to hit me you know?" Carson asked, his voice even quieter, his eyes boring into the ground. "Before he got crippled in the accident."

I continued to dab at the welts.

"He was a real bastard," he continued. "To me and my mom. Out of nowhere...*pop*. You know? For nothing. You didn't have to do anything to set him off. But I miss him. And I hate him. But I'm glad he's dead because I'm fucking exhausted."

Though I'd applied plenty of calamine to Carson's welts, I kept dabbing here and there so that I could pretend I wasn't meeting his eyes due to my focus on his wounds. I think he knew that.

"It's hard, you know? Being a kid and people expecting you to do shit like take care of your crippled father," he murmured. "No one really helping out. Asking if you have enough to eat or anything. Not caring if the roof of your shitbox house leaks in the middle of the night and wakes you up so you spend half the night fixing the leak and then you're exhausted for school the next day. As soon as you get home you can't take a nap because the little help you have can't stick around to give you one fucking moment of goddamn peace. You never feel rested. Ever."

I flipped the lid of the bottle shut and set it carefully next to me. Staring down at the cracked and dry earth, I said nothing.

"I'm glad he's dead," Carson said. "So I can live. And I feel like shit for it."

With a sigh, and a bubbling of anger in my gut that I hadn't known was waiting to be addressed, I looked up at Carson.

"Do you thuh-think I shuh-should feel sorry for you?" I asked.

Carson shook his head.

"I duh-don't."

"Good," Carson said.

"You wuh-were a shithead," I said. "You tuh-tortured me, Cuh-Carson. You were a fuuuh-fucking dick."

He nodded down at the ground, refusing to meet my eyes.

"So, fuh-fuck you," I said.

Again, he nodded.

With a sigh, my shoulders slumped, and the fire that had threatened to spew up from my gut and out of me...gave up. I was exhausted, too.

"I'm suh-orry about your dad," I said, finally. "And fuck huh-im, too."

Carson said nothing, and I had nothing more to say. Leaning my head back, I looked up at the few wisps of clouds like cotton candy in the azure sky. The sun was white hot, but it wasn't nearly as warm as it had been in recent months. I desperately wanted those clouds to get their act together. To work as a team. The earth was exhausted as well.

"Are we going back to my house now?" Carson asked quietly.

There was no point in thinking about it.

"Yeah," I said.

Chapter 15

CARSON

Kevin's left arm and leg were draped over me when the thunder shook the walls of the house. When my eyes shot open, the house was pitch black and the walls were still trembling from the force of the sound. A streak of lightning turned the threadbare white curtains into boxes of white-hot light. The room filled with light, then was pitched into utter darkness once more. Glancing over at Kevin, and finding his eyes shut tightly, I shimmied out from underneath him and lowered my feet to the bare wood floor.

I tiptoed from my room, still nude, and into the living room. Out on the porch, naked to the world, I looked out through the darkness. A rumble in the distance made a shiver crawl up my spine. I turned my head skyward at the edge of the porch and found only inky blackness waiting. Still as a graveyard, not even a breeze whistled over the trees.

Out of nowhere, a silent streak of lightning shot through the sky. No longer black, the lightning illuminated the heavy, angry looking gray clouds above. The rumbling of thunder followed as the sky turned black again.

"What is it?" Kevin asked sleepily behind me. "I heard thuh-thunder."

He tiptoed up to stand beside me on the porch, naked as well.

"I think it might actually rain," I whispered, my eyes still on the sky.

"Really?"

Another streak of lightning, accompanied by a clap of thunder so violent we both jumped, answered for me. Kevin's eyes looked gray in the flash of light as he stared up at the sky with wonder. Then the lightning was gone and the wood boards under our feet slowly stopped trembling.

"A ruh-real storm," Kevin said, simply.

"It might be a bad one." I agreed.

"Do you thuh-think..."

Kevin trailed off, but I knew what he was thinking.

"Maybe," I said. "This is going to be bad, though. If it's enough to fill the creek."

"Yeah."

"My roof might leak," I said. "It probably will."

I hadn't wanted to say that out loud—to admit out loud that my house was a shitbox—though we both knew it. It wouldn't have been fair not to warn Kevin, though.

"Okay," he said. "We'll duh-deal wuh-with it."

"Okay," I replied. "Let's...let's get inside."

Another clap of thunder and a streak of lightning chased us back across the porch and into the house. We crawled back into bed, and at first, tried to go back to sleep. Side by side we laid in bed nude, waiting for the lightning that flashed in the windows and the thunder that shook the house to drop buckets on the inadequate roof above. When the wind began to howl and the lightning was like strobe lights, we pulled on our clothes and moved to the living room to wait.

In the darkness of the pre-dawn hours, we waited. When a clap of thunder rattled the house so violently that I thought it might shake apart, and a flash of lightning turned the living room brilliant white, I expected to hear rain. Only silence followed. The living room felt humid and sticky. Suffocating and electric.

For several minutes, we sat in silence and darkness, wondering if the storm had decided against providing the relief we so desperately needed. Minutes later, when I was considering suggesting we simply go back to bed, the first drops of rain sounded on the roof.

At first it was an infrequent "tick-tack" sound that slowly picked up. Soon it sounded like the sky was simply dumping the contents of every cloud directly onto my roof. The leaks began immediately. Kevin and I rushed around the house, putting plastic tubs, pots, pans, and anything that could hold water under the dozens of leaks throughout my tiny little house. When they filled, which happened quickly, one of us would race the container out to the porch and toss it out into the deluge, then rush it back inside to put under the leak once more.

For hours, Kevin and I fought against the leaks, though as the rain calmed to a slow, steady downpour, we were able to catch a breath occasionally. It wasn't until the curtains in the windows turned luminescent gray with early morning light shining through clouds that we were able to ignore the buckets for more than a few minutes.

Out on the porch, fully clothed this time, we watched the rain spatters and assessed the swamp that now surrounded my house. Kevin laid a hand on my shoulder and squeezed it as I looked up to find several slats in the porch roof missing. Obviously, they had been knocked into the yard, but the mud was such that they would be impossible to find until the rain abated and the yard dried up some. Probably within a few days. If we were lucky.

It just depended on the rain.

"This will take forever to fix," I mumbled. "I don't have the money."

Kevin squeezed my shoulder again.

Chapter 16
CARSON

Downtown flooded. Kevin and I walked from my house into town to check out the damage caused by the storm. Though the water was receding on the main street, it was as if a new creek had formed and was flowing directly through town. Wallace Lee and his employees were doing their best to use push brooms to help the standing inch of water out of the front door of the Sav-A-Ton. We did our best to avoid his notice, in case he saw us and begged for help. It wasn't that we didn't want to help, but helping meant we would be kept from continuing on our mission to check out the entire town.

The old-timers hadn't taken up their posts outside the convenience store to watch everything and whisper to each other about all of it. I imagined they were still at home, surveying the damage done to their own property. Then again, the gray sky was still spitting a hazy mist. It wasn't enough to really add to the damage already done, but it was enough of an annoyance to keep people indoors if they had no good reason to get out.

Ralph and Shirley were a mirror image of Wallace Lee and his employees. Push brooms were being utilized to help the deluge recede from their store. Small wave after small wave of water gushed from the front door of the convenience store as they did their best to clean up the mess from the storm. Ralph was carrying on, sputtering with frustration when Kevin and I walked by.

That's it. It was the air conditioner. Then those cracks. Now we got a leakin' roof and a swimmin' pool. I'm sellin' off to that fella, Shirls. I'm tellin' ya'! I will NOT hush up. I'm 'bout tired of—

With a chuckle, Kevin and I ducked around the convenience store out of sight. We didn't want to help Shirley and Ralph, either. Though I felt sorry for Wallace Lee and Shirley and Ralph—my place was going to need massive repairs and the money to do them was nonexistent—I still felt light. The misty morning, the rain we had desperately needed, felt like it was washing away a summer I'd be happy to forget.

Furtively, the two of us wound our way through Podunk, taking in the damage around town. Some houses had obviously taken damage to their roof shingles. Limbs lay in yards, some having landed on and damaged fences, cars, and out buildings. A few windows hadn't stood up to debris tossed about by the wind. The gutters on the residential streets were still a torrent of flood water, gushing along, carrying debris and garbage.

Kevin's and my hair was plastered to our heads and our shirts clung to our chests from the mist, but we continued to walk. It was still early in the day, so other than Wallace Lee and Shirley and Ralph, not many people had even begun addressing the damages caused by the storm. I figured that until the mist stopped spitting from the sky, and it was certain the storm had passed, no one would bother. Temporary repairs to windows and leaking roofs would be done, but tree limbs on fences could wait for the sun to come out again.

After surveying town, Kevin and I found ourselves clomping through the now swamp-like woods. The desperately thirsty ground had been too dry to soak up the water quickly, so we trudged through mud and standing water on our way to the creek. The trees seemed to shiver appreciatively, soaking up the mist and enjoying the coolness of the day. I didn't know if the woods were trying to come back to life, but alive is what I felt.

We heard the creek before we arrived. A gushing sound, like a waterfall or white rapids, greeted our ears at least fifty yards from the creek. Moments later, when we had traversed that last bit of distance, we found that the bank of the creek was further back than it had ever been. A great, angry ribbon of flood water slashed through the clearing in the woods. The creek had almost widened from one tree line to the other on either side.

Swiftly moving, brown and sludgy, the creek was dangerous. Tree limbs and other debris rushed by in the tide of water as Kevin and I stood just beyond the tree line and stared at the creek in awe. It should have been frightening, seeing the creek we used to swim in on lazy summer days appear so forceful and angry, but it simply felt renewed. The water would eventually recede a bit. Settle. The creek water would clear. Kids would be able to swim in it again. Maybe not until next summer, but things would return to normal. If we waited.

"Jeez," Kevin whispered.

"Yeah," I said, unable to keep the smile from my face.

"This is cuh-razy," Kevin said.

When he turned to me, he didn't look scared. He was smiling. Almost impishly. I grinned back.

The sky sputtered, a quick burst of rain that slapped against our faces, then settled back into a mist. Maybe it was actually the trees above shedding water that had collected on their branches. Kevin chuckled and closed his eyes as the rain poured down his face. When he opened his eyes, smiling at me,

I reached out and put my hand to his forehead, pushing his hair back.

Laughing, he reached out and returned the gesture.

Though I had no idea why, I found my arms raising and my hands finding his biceps. I pulled him into me and pressed my lips to his. Rain slithered down our faces as I held my mouth against his. The rush of the creek and my pulse thudded in my ears as I kissed Kevin right there in the middle of the rain in the woods.

When Kevin suddenly pushed me away, nearly causing me to stumble into the creek, my eyes grew wide. The push had been so violent that I expected to look up and find Kevin seething with rage. Instead, I found that he was staring at me quizzically.

"Kevin—"

He didn't wait to listen.

He turned and dashed off into the woods from the direction we'd come.

And I was left with only the creek flooding my ears. Because I was certain my heart had stopped beating in my chest.

Chapter 17

KEVIN

"You might as well know," Ralph announced grandly, "I'm gonna sell this godforsaken place."

The door had barely swung shut behind the customer I'd just cashed out and told to "have a nice day" when my boss spoke up. Pushing the cash drawer closed with my hip, like I'd done a million times over the course of my employment at the convenience store, I turned to face him. Proud of his announcement, Ralph was grinning widely. I wasn't certain how I felt about his and Shirley's decision to offload the store once and for all. I couldn't blame them. It was turning into a money pit.

But where would I work?

Did I even care?

It was possible it was time to move on and his decision to sell the store was the poke in the behind that I needed to find something else. I could finally get off my ass and put my degree to use. At the very least, I'd never tiptoe into the house and hear my dad bitching about my lack of ambition.

"Wh-when?" I asked.

Ralph straightened up.

"I'm gonna go over there and talk to Wallace Lee right now," he said. "He wants this place so bad, he can buy it. Take over the whole damn town. I don't care."

"Okay."

I didn't know what else to say, so I didn't say much. That only confused Ralph. His smile faltered for a minute, but with obvious effort, he forced himself to continue smiling. He marched to the front door, resolute in his decision. Before pushing the front door wide, he turned to me again.

"I'll make sure he does you and Danielle right, Kevin," he announced grandly, as though he was doing me the highest of favors.

"Okay."

My continued lack of interest further eroded Ralph's enthusiasm. Frowning, his mouth screwed up with concern. He started to say something, but instead, pushed the door open and dashed out into the cool early autumn day.

I couldn't help but smile at the soft breeze that blew through the store, rustling the small bags of chips hung from the endcap by the door. Autumn was finally chasing away the straggling remains of the worst summer we'd ever seen. Soon, the skeletal trees would look festive instead of foreboding.

With nothing better to do and a lack of customers, I set about my cleaning duties. Wiping down the counters and cleaning around the register turned into taking apart and cleaning all the soda fountains. That turned into cleaning out the drink cases and dusting and organizing the product shelves. I was on my hands and knees, cleaning along the baseboards and under the display cases when Ralph breezed back into the store, nearly slamming the door into the wall as he made his way inside.

"*I'll be in my office!*" he announced loudly, not bothering to stop and chat.

Well, what's done is done. I had thought to myself, pausing only briefly to consider my future before going back to cleaning.

The day flew by without another word from Ralph. He didn't even leave his office. When a business owner decides to sell, I assume they spend time going over finances and dog-earing their future windfall for all the luxuries they plan to splurge on. Then again, I couldn't imagine that Ralph would end up wealthy with the sale of the store, but I was no expert.

I still hadn't seen Ralph or heard a peep from him when Danielle came into the store for her shift that afternoon. Whispering to each other, I gave her the gist of the day's events. Whether or not Ralph would give her the same courtesy bestowed upon me was unclear, so I wanted to make sure she wouldn't be blindsided by the news.

Danielle's reaction was similar to mine. With a shrug of her shoulders, she said she'd wait and see if Wallace Lee wanted her to stay on. If not, she'd simply have to find a new place to underpay her. We both shared a conspiratorial laugh, and I slipped out of the store.

Outdoors, I immediately felt tense. I no longer had the four walls of the store to hide within or the register to hide behind. I felt exposed. Though I knew I wouldn't run into Carson if I stuck to the streets of town—or, at least, it would be unlikely I'd run into him—I was concerned. Going home to ensure my safety presented its own problem in my parents.

So, minutes later, I found myself out at the creek. Not at the spot where Carson and I always met up, but further upstream. Far enough away from our meeting spot that he wouldn't see me if he ventured out to stand on the banks of the creek. Still moving too rapidly to be safe to swim in, though the water was clearing a bit and receding further from the tree line, the creek was still violent. I had no idea how long it takes a creek to resettle after a big storm, but the mushy ground underfoot led me to believe it would take a bit of time.

I stayed there, leaning against a tree, staring at the creek for so long that the sun was beginning to set when I decided it was time to leave. The roaring water, cast golden by the setting sun, was my own personal symphony as I made my way back into the woods.

Going home still held no appeal, so I went to the only other place where I knew that I could avoid everything.

As expected, Wallace Lee was relaxing in his metal clamshell lawn chair in his backyard when I peeked around the corner of his house. Unlike the other times I'd visited him over the summer, the air carried no sound of buzzing bees. I stood at the corner of his house and stared out at the edge of the woods. The mobile garden was still there, but not a single bee was buzzing around the white chest of drawers contraption that had been their temporary home.

"One bit of rain and those bees act like the world's been handed back to them on a silver platter," Wallace Lee said, drawing my attention.

Amused, he shook his head and lifted his beer to his lips. I shuffled over and settled into the chair next to him. For a few moments we sat there, him sipping his beer, neither of us saying anything.

"Wuh-where are they now?" I asked.

He sucked at his teeth.

"I suspect they went back to their own hive," he said. "That's what I imagine anyway. It's gettin' colder, so...well, I don't know what that means for bees. Those students came and saw that they'd abandoned the hive out there, so they've lost interest. Didn't stick around long enough for me to ask too many questions."

I nodded.

"I guess they're doing whatever bees do when summer's over," he said. "Those kids said they'd come remove the hive and garden next week. Too busy today, I suppose."

"Yeah."

"Can't say I'll miss seein' those kids out there messin' around, but I'll miss hearin' the bees," he said. "It was kind of nice sittin' out here in the early evening, listenin' to 'em. Now I just got my own thoughts and those don't sound so sweet sometimes."

"Yeah."

"What's crawled up your butt?" Wallace Lee chuckled. "You forget how to talk?"

A rueful smile crossed my lips, but I had no idea what to say. Or if I even had anything to say. And if I did, did I want to say it?

"I don't know," I managed to say.

"Well," Wallace Lee said slowly, "I guess sometimes bein' quiet is a good thing. I could probably practice that myself sometimes."

He chuckled. I smiled.

Several more minutes ticked by as the two of us sat there, listening to the silence. We watched as the sky turned from a hazy gold to pink, violet, and purple. I wasn't certain how much time passed as we sat there, but stars were beginning to peek through that purple when Wallace Lee spoke again.

"Why ain't you out there with Carson? Playin' wild boys of the woods?"

I knew that Wallace Lee's comment was probably innocent. However, his tone made me wonder if he didn't have suspicions about what had transpired over the previous weeks—for all of summer, really. That was something I definitely didn't want to say.

"Duh-dunno."

"I've been waitin' for him to show up at the store," he said. "I'm ready to give him a job whenever he's ready. But I guess grieving takes time."

I nodded; said nothing.

"It's hard to change a way of livin'," Wallace Lee sighed. "Like the bees. You can't force nothin'."

"Yeah."

Wallace Lee lifted his beer, realized it was empty when he tried to take a sip, then dropped it next to his chair. He sat forward, propping his arms on his knees.

"You know bees pick flowers based on the length of their tongues?"

I turned to look at Wallace Lee. I couldn't help but smile.

"Bees with longer tongues can get nectar from flowers like honeysuckle, and those with shorter tongues will go for daisies and whatnot," he explained. "Of course, I guess, the ones with longer tongues can go to any flower they like. It's the ones with shorter tongues that have to be picky."

Staring off at the woods, my eyes fixed on the empty hive.

"But I figure that all bees try every flower they can until they figure out the ones that work best for them. Sometimes they get the right flowers and sometimes they get the wrong flowers, but they keep tryin'. 'Cause that's what bees were meant to do."

"Bees don't live long," I said quietly. "What if they spend their whole life trying the wrong flowers?"

Wallace Lee watched me for a moment, his eyes boring into the side of my head. I refused to look at him. Finally, after several uncomfortable moments, he sat back in his chair and laid his hands comfortably on the arms of his chair.

"I suppose you have to wonder if you can ever choose the wrong flower if there's a chance of makin' honey," Wallace Lee said.

I sighed. A tension I didn't realize I was carrying in my shoulders disappeared and I felt my body relaxing into the chair.

"I'm nothin' special, son," Wallace Lee said, sucking at his teeth again. "I'm not a philosopher or a great mind or nothin' like that. But I'm not dumb. I got some sense about me. Mostly for business, but I also know a little about life. I've always felt that as it is with the bees, so is it with boys, that they are never more alive than when they answer the wildness that calls from within. At least for as long as it calls."

Finally, my head turned so I could meet Wallace Lee's eyes.

"We're all out here tryin' to make honey," he said. "Because that's what somethin' inside of us tells us to do. From the moment we take our first breath until we gasp our last one. We can't help it. Sometimes we find flowers that work and sometimes we have to try again. But never say a flower was wrong if you were just tryin' to make honey. Because tryin' to make honey is what makes us feel alive. And sometimes feelin' alive is all we got. Ya' hear me?"

Nodding, I turned my attention back to the woods.

"Yes, sir," I said.

Wallace Lee slapped at his knee and laughed, then suddenly turned serious.

"It's been a minute since someone in this town said a 'yes, sir' to me," he said quietly, his head turning to stare off towards the woods as well.

I expected him to launch into a story, but as I was, Wallace Lee stared off at the woods. The darkness was encroaching on us before I found the nerve to speak.

"Wallace—"

"That boy," Wallace Lee interrupted me, "took a part of this town with him."

I didn't have to ask who he was talking about.

Wallace Lee sighed, sat back, and laid his hands on the arms of the chair again, though his eyes stayed fixed on the woods.

"He knew he wasn't slick," Wallace Lee said. "He knew that I knew he was stealing food from my store. I caught him several times. Never said nothin', neither. Just made sure I kept the things he took most in stock. At first, I thought he was takin' care of him and his momma. God knows they needed the help."

I nodded. Ian had definitely needed help, even if he'd never have taken any.

"But he was takin' food to your friend out there," Wallace Lee said. "Makin' sure him and his daddy were fed. Kept nothin' for himself. Well…maybe some sunflower seeds."

He chuckled.

"But never much. People in this town don't take care of each other like that. They don't care if the people wither and rot and the town falls down around them. As long as things stay the same. They'd go without honey just to make sure certain people stay in their place. They hate other people more than they love themselves."

I felt a tear threaten to escape the corner of my eye, but I willed it away.

"I don't know how that boy ever survived. Either of them boys," Wallace Lee said quietly. "It's a damn miracle they did— and they owe not a damn soul gratitude for it because they did it on their own. To this day, I'm damned ashamed I didn't do more for either of them. But I looked the other way when I could."

"The food huh-elped so much, Wallace Lee," I said. "That wasn't nuh-nothing."

Again, he was sucking at his teeth and a bitter, angry look crossed his face.

"I wish I could thank you for that sentiment," he said. "But it wasn't concern over what people in this town would think if I helped Carson out. His daddy killed my wife."

Frozen, I stared at the side of Wallace Lee's head as he glared out at the woods.

"Both those boys had daddies that weren't worth the salt in my tears," Wallace Lee spat. "And I ain't cryin' over either of 'em bein' gone. Never before have two more worthless, despicable men ever walked this earth."

I swallowed hard.

"Both drinkers, wife beaters—beat their kids—caroused, cheated, lied, stole…*worthless sumbitches*. Both of 'em. I'm glad they're both gone."

"Cuh-arson's dad—"

"Wreck that put him up in that chair killed my wife," Wallace Lee sniffed, but it wasn't sadness. It was derision. "Killed his wife, too. For a long time, I felt that was justice, but she was a good woman. She just had a worthless husband. She should've been left and him gone. But like that other worthless sumbitch, his drinkin' ruined lives. And I'm glad that sumbitch is now dead. I've been waitin' a long time to say that."

I lowered my head to look at the grass, nearly black under the night sky.

"But my anger at him still bein' alive kept me from helpin' that boy directly," Wallace Lee said. "I ain't sorry that evil sumbitch is dead, but I'm sorry for only lookin' the other way when food was stolen. I could've done more. I'm sorry that, like the rest of this town, I looked away the whole time both of those boys were sufferin'. We all deserve to be ashamed and to get whatever comes our way."

He sat back in his chair with finality. That was all Wallace Lee had to say. I let him sit with his thoughts for a few moments before speaking.

"The fuh-food wasn't nuh-nothing," I said. "It was m...ore than anyone else duh-did for him."

"Maybe so," Wallace Lee said, and turned to smile softly at me, "but let me hate on myself for a little while. I've earned it."

I chuckled softly.

Mirroring Wallace Lee's position, I sat back in the chair and laid my hands on the arms. The sky was now ink speckled with silver and a cool breeze whistled through his backyard. I felt that if I listened closely enough, I'd probably be able to hear the creek roaring in the woods. I had no idea how long it would take for the creek to subside and return to normal, but in the meantime, at least it was no longer empty.

"Duh-id Ralph sell the store to yuh-you today?" I asked.

"He did not."

Frowning, I asked, "Why not? He suh-said he was going to."

"I don't want it," Wallace Lee waved me off. "I got enough on my plate. And I'm not gettin' any younger. Buyin' another store? Nah. I want to retire one day. I'm not lookin' to make myself busier."

He chuckled, so I chuckled with him.

"Seems to me that no one will want to buy that store from him if I don't," Wallace Lee said cryptically. "He'll just have to run it until he's too damned old to do it anymore."

I figured Wallace Lee was right. Who wants to own a convenience store in Podunk?

"Unless he sells it cheap to someone," Wallace Lee added. "Between you and me, I wouldn't feel sorry for Ralph and Shirley if they sold it cheap. They've made enough money off this town."

My head turned automatically to stare at Wallace Lee.

"If someone got a loan from someone—a silent partner, maybe?" He shrugged, his shoulders rising and falling in the darkness. "Buy Ralph and Shirley out? They could work and pay back that loan and become a full owner. That'd be a nice little business for someone who plans to live and work around here. It ain't the type of place to make retiring in the Bahamas money, but it'd be good livin' around here. Like my grocery store."

It felt like my heart was doing hopscotch in my chest. My mind was racing.

"Who knows? Things the way they are, you never know when industry is going to move in. One day, this tiny little worthless town might be ten times this size. It's happening all over. Maybe, one day, that little store could make retiring in Bahamas money. Who's to say? This town might be worth somethin' one day. If the right people are driving the car."

Wallace Lee turned his head, grinned, and winked at me.

"But I don't know of anyone that would be interested," he said. "Do you?"

"I—"

"Might even be a good business for co-owners," he interrupted. "Yeah. Co-owners. Can't afford employees right away? Take turns runnin' shifts. And where one head is good, two is better. Double the ideas."

I turned to look out at the woods again, though I could barely see them in the dark. My mind raced as a grin pricked at the corner of my mouth. A grin of possibility.

"Yeah," Wallace Lee sighed. "That sounds right. That would be a good plan. I think it's time I stopped lookin' the other way."

My smile grew.

Chapter 18

CARSON

Giving up was all I could do. Boards from the porch roof lay in a pile in the front yard alongside the pile of shingles I'd pried from the roof. I hadn't had a chance to really inspect all of the boards in the roof that would need to be replaced. But that was a hopeless chore. Even if I could figure out where all the leaks were, I'd never be able to afford the lumber. My house was a lost cause.

It was possible that I could gather some tarps and secure them to keep any rain out that might come, but that was a temporary solution. It would be good enough until fixes could be made, but without being able to afford the material to make the fixes, it was pointless. Within weeks, my house would be completely uninhabitable. Though the rain had been nonexistent through summer, one good storm always turns up another.

I didn't know how long it would be before it rained again, but it could never hold off long enough. Praying for another drought would have been irresponsible anyway. Life had had its way with me and I had to accept it. My house was in shambles, not that it had ever been anything grand to begin with, and there was no way around it.

I wanted to punch through a wall. Throw shit. But it was pointless. And my heart wouldn't have really been in it anyway. That was the old me, threatening an outburst to deal with life.

I was no longer that person.

But I had no idea who I was, either.

There was no one who needed me. No plan. No clear path forward.

So, I dropped the hammer I'd been holding, sending it clattering atop the boards laid haphazardly around my feet on the porch. I walked over to the edge of the porch, eased myself down, and sat there, my legs dangling, grazing the tops of the weeds below.

With a sigh, I stared out blankly at the craggy yard, still swampy from the storm. The ground was slowly soaking up and absorbing all of the rain we'd gotten. Things would dry out soon enough. If we didn't get more rain within the next few days.

I'd have to get a job. Find a place to live. Figure out how I was going to move forward when there was no clear path laid out before me. The only thing that kept me from feeling hopeless was that I was unencumbered. Anything was possible.

Maybe I'd go see Wallace Lee again. Claim the job he said he'd keep waiting for me. Working at the grocery store would be good enough for the time being. Maybe…if the rain held out…I could work enough, make enough money, to fix the house before it totally collapsed around me. If the timing was right, it was possible I could save the house.

If that's what I decided I wanted.

Podunk didn't present a lot of options for housing, but I could see what all was possible. I simply had to get up, start taking steps, and see where my feet led.

Sighing, I lowered my eyes.

It would be hard figuring everything out on my own. Even though Dad had never been much for helping make decisions and couldn't help with everything that had to be accomplished from day to day, at least I hadn't been alone.

For the first time in my entire life, I was alone.

I wasn't sure if that scared me or liberated me.

But I knew that I preferred not being alone, regardless.

As if summoned by my thoughts, I heard him walking down the mostly overgrown trail that led to the house. I didn't dare smile as I lifted my head and turned to watch him walking up into the yard.

Kevin's expression was guarded as much as my own, but he met my eyes and didn't falter. He walked right up, stopping a few yards away from me. For several moments, we simply stared at each other. It had never occurred to me before how well Kevin and I could do silence. It meant nothing and everything. And it was always comfortable.

Since he had come out to the house on his own, I waited for him to speak.

Finally, he said: "A lot of damage?"

"Yeah," I said. "It's...yeah. It might be a loss. I don't know yet."

He nodded slowly.

"I can maybe do some temporary fixes. I don't know. I need to go get a job. Make some money. See what I can do. Maybe I can beat the clock, you know? Fix it before another storm finishes the job."

I chuckled ruefully and he joined in.

"You nuh-know," Kevin said, "I was thinking. About yuh-your house. And mine."

"Yeah?"

"My puh-arents kind of suck," he said. "But whose duh-don't?"

I couldn't help but grin at that.

"May…be it's tuh-time for me to find my own puh-place," he said. "Or maybe guh-get a ruh-roommate."

I just watched him.

"I have muh-money," he continued. "You nuh-eed money. I need to move. You huh-have a spuh-spuh-are ruh-room."

He shrugged.

I considered what Kevin was suggesting, though I'd already made up my mind as he was speaking. However, nothing is ever that simple.

"Kevin," I said, "the other day, I—"

"It's nuh-not who wuh-we are," he said.

He wasn't stopping me or making sure I didn't try to make a case for what I'd done. He knew what I was going to say. He was agreeing with me. We weren't those guys. We were friends. Soon to be roommates. The rest had served its purpose. That was all.

I gave him an upward nod.

"Suh-so?" he asked. "What duh-do you say?"

"Roommates would be great," I said automatically. "I like that idea."

He smiled. "Okay."

"When do you want to—"

"I want to guh-go inside," Kevin said, cutting me off. "One luh-last time. Before I muh-move in. Buh-before we're ruh-roommates."

Something inside of me told me that deep down I'd been hoping he'd suggest that.

"Just once more," I said.

He nodded.

"Do I still make you nervous?" I asked, grinning. "You're still stuttering a lot."

Kevin didn't smile at my joke. He didn't react at all. Instead, he looked off in the direction from which he came. The seconds that passed, the silence he let us steep in, nearly drove me crazy. But I waited.

"Suh-some puh-people will always make a guh-guy nervous," he said finally. "But it's nuh-not for the ruh-wrong reasons anymore."

Somehow, that made perfect sense.

I rose to stand before him on the porch, my excitement already evident. With a crook of my head, I welcomed him to come up the steps. Kevin said nothing but immediately walked those last few yards to the porch and clomped up the steps. His brow was furrowed and his mouth seemed tense with unspoken thoughts.

"You look like you have a bee in your bonnet," I said.

He chuckled faintly. "I'll tuh-tell you luh-later. When we cuh-come back out-suh-side.'"

"Okay," I said.

Kevin led the way inside and I shut the door behind us. Once inside the dark, cool house, Kevin turned to me, that tension and worry in his face no longer there. When he stepped up to me and softly pressed his lips to mine, I didn't stop him. It was just a small, quick, but thorough kiss, yet it held meaning. When he pulled back, he ran a thumb over my lips. Brushed my hair back from my forehead.

I stared into his eyes as he reached for my shirttail and lifted it, pulling it off over my head. Kissing his way down my body, I watched as he hooked his fingers to my jeans button and began to undress the lower half of me. For several minutes, once my pants were gone, Kevin took his time bringing me to the brink of ecstasy, stopping as it became evident that continuing would end things.

He rose from his kneeling position and led me to my room. And, for the first time, Kevin pushed me down on the bed. I laid there, waiting excitedly for him as he undressed himself and climbed up onto the bed. Nervous when he began to lift my legs to his shoulders, I still found that I desperately wanted to experience the thing that only Kevin had gotten to experience over our summer together.

As the minutes and hours ticked by, I began to realize that Kevin hadn't meant "just once more." He'd meant "one more night." I found that I was fine with that. Maybe it wasn't who we were going to be, but for the time being, it made me realize that who I was could change.

And that was exactly what I needed.

Chapter 19

KEVIN

We didn't go back outside until the sun had fallen and rose once again. Neither of had slept, but if we had, it was only briefly. Instead, we spent the night trying to make honey, even if we knew it would prove pointless in the end. Well, maybe not pointless, but we both knew we were the wrong flowers. The time we'd spent discovering that hadn't been a waste, because it had made us both feel alive.

We'd answered that wild thing inside of us that demanded we live.

That was never pointless.

And it had been fun. It had been the whisper of hope during a cruel summer.

When the rising sun had turned the curtains golden, Carson and I were side by side in his bed, breathless, sweaty, and smiling. Every time we looked at each other, we chuckled. Things would be okay. He still made me nervous, but it wasn't because he was Carson. It was because I finally understood who he was. To me.

Carson excused himself to the bathroom, so I slipped into my underwear and wrapped his blanket around me. Outside, the sun looked red through the trees as it began its journey over the horizon. I sat down on the porch, pulling the blanket tightly around myself to ward off the chilly autumn morning.

Weeds tickled at the soles of my feet as my legs dangled from the porch.

Though I knew Carson and I were leaving behind the adventure we'd begun in summer, I couldn't help but smile as I waited for the coming day. There was another adventure to share ahead and more things to discover. There was no point in mourning an adventure that has ended when you shared it with the right person.

"It's chilly," Carson mumbled as he stepped through the door and padded across the porch.

He plopped down next to me, rubbing his upper arms.

"I guess autumn is finally here, huh?" he asked.

"Yeah."

He nudged me.

"Are roommates allowed to share blankets?" He teased.

"Yeah." I laughed. "Ruh-roommates can share buh-lankets."

I pulled the blanket free from around my body and Carson scooted over so that we could drape it around both of us as best we could. Our sides were touching, but neither of us pulled the other in closer. And it didn't feel awkward. We were simply sharing the warmth of the blanket. I could actually feel the closure between the two of us.

That was over now.

Though I felt a bit sad, it also felt right. I realized that maybe sadness didn't necessarily have to be a bad thing.

"When are you going to move in?" Carson asked softly.

I shrugged.

"Today?"

He laughed. "Ready to get out of the parents' house that badly, huh?"

Nodding, I laughed with him. "You huh-have no idea."

We both watched the sun rise beyond the trees and into the sky.

"You can have my dad's old room. We never really used it much. Not after the accident."

"Okay."

Sitting there in amiable silence, I began to realize that it might actually be a cold day. Not just a chilly morning. Even with the sun rising into the sky, it wasn't chasing away the chill. Carson shivered at my side, letting me know that he was probably having the same thought. I didn't mind the cold. We'd had enough summer.

It's funny how that happens. The harshest seasons make it easier to let go of what was so that we can move on to the next.

"Then what?" Carson asked quietly.

I wasn't sure he was actually asking me or simply talking out loud.

We find a new flower to make our honey, I thought to myself with a smile.

"What is it?" Carson nudged me.

He had noticed my smile. When I turned to look at him, he was smiling at me playfully. Then he nudged me again, eliciting a laugh.

I said, "I've guh-got a really guh-good idea. Well, someone guh-gave me a really good idea."

"I'm dying to hear it," Carson grinned.

The End.

A Note from Chase about
'A Species of Special Concern'

I wrote *The Bees and Other Wild Things* a few years ago, though I never considered publishing it until my developmental editor convinced me. Before that happened, however, I wanted to give readers who fell in love with Ian Chambers and Michael Steedman a special treat. So, I wrote *A Species of Special Concern*. It's a short story that takes place after the events of *The Bees and Other Wild Things*.

It was on my website for over a year, free to read. I present it now, here, at the back of this book for your further enjoyment. So that you can read it anytime you want on your e-reader or in paperback format anytime the mood strikes you.

Now that you've read both *A Surplus of Light* and *The Bees and Other Wild Things*, maybe it will be different. So, if you've already read it, a second reading will help give it deeper meaning. If you are reading it for the first time, I hope you enjoy it. If it's not your first time reading it, I hope you enjoy it even more the second time around.

Regardless, thank you all for joining me in another writing adventure with four characters I thoroughly enjoyed bringing to life and sharing with all of you.

Spending time with all of you will always be one of the greatest joys in my life.

Tremendous Love & Thanks,
Chase

A Species
of
Special Concern

Golden grass, like butterscotch glistening in the sun, the kind that only the dog days of August can produce, scratched at my shoulder blades. Parched and crackly from the late days of summer, the grass whispered its symphony as I stretched lazily under the sympathetic shade of the Live Oak. Motes danced in sunlight as it snuck through the canopy of leaves above us; sweltering, hazy, yellow beams invaded our sanctuary beneath the tree. My eyes opened and closed languidly as his head rested upon my chest, rising and falling with each of my respirations.

Sweat trickled from his brow onto my bare skin, but I didn't care. Rivulets of streaky liquid salt would dry and decorate my skin for the remainder of the day. A proclamation of proof that *we were here. We are still here. We will always be…here.* A part of us would always be here, at least. Languidly, my eyes opened and closed as I reached to his forehead and brushed the sweat-soaked hair back off of his brow. He smiled in his fraudulent sleep, no longer capable of pretending he had drifted off when he felt my fingertips against his sunbaked skin. He crooked his head just so and his eyes slid open as a satiated, lazy smile overtook his visage.

Continuing its chorus, the grass sang under us as he shifted, bringing his mouth to mine. A gentle—yet passionate—ephemeral kiss before the dewy skin on the side of his face laid upon my chest once again. With a sigh, I brought both of my arms up to lace my fingers under my head, my own sweat-drenched hair slick against the flesh of my palms.

If this was the best that life could be, it was more than I'd ever hoped.

Since dawn, as nature performed its aubade, we had walked the fields and woods, walked the water's edge, held hands, didn't hold hands, snuck away into the deepest, coolest, most remote parts of the woods where our bodies became one. We chuckled throatily as we lay there, naked and sweaty, our limbs intertwined under the shadowy darkness of the jungle of our youth. Together we glowed in the deepest reaches of the woods, never wanting to untangle ourselves from each other. As all things go, there was more to do than just bask in the afterglow.

When the morning surrendered to the afternoon, we had assailed the insulated picnic bag and dined like kings upon chips and sandwiches, tea and lemonade. This was our kingdom once again—*if only for a brief while*—and we lorded over it as only those determined to relive the hubris of their youth are wont to do. Our kingdom had received no worthy impugning kings or queens in the years of our absence, and we had wasted no time in reclaiming our lands. Our power was absolute, and we set out on our adventure.

Hiking and frolicking, peals of laughter echoing off of the trees around us. Dashing around trees, giving chase, as though the ultimate goal was not to be caught. Our bare feet trod upon firm summer earth, turned up by the rains of spring, then packed down tightly by the feet of travelers that had been by earlier in the summer. Our toes scrunched up in the grass deep in the woods that was still green and carpet-like since it had not been baked by the unrelenting hot summer sun. Our naked bodies explored that grass more than our toes did as we rolled across it during our lovemaking. And it had decorated our hair like confetti afterward until it was brushed away with laughter and grit-covered fingers.

Home.

Though I knew it to be false—some olfactory memory casting its illusion upon me—I smelled the acrid, yet sweet, smell of flowering vines as we laid under the Live Oak. It brought a smile to my face as I remembered patches of light searching out and dancing along our bodies years before—when we had laid naked in the woods in our youth. Just as it was doing now as we laid together, shirtless and unapologetically carefree under the tree, and crunchy grass serenaded us, beckoning us to slumber. Though, this time, we had shown enough propriety to keep our shorts on.

"Do you hear that?" He asked quietly, his lips fluttering against the skin of my chest.

"What?"

"Memories," he said. "That's what that sound is. *Memories.*"

I smiled. "Memories make good music."

He nuzzled his face in my chest playfully, the slight stubble of his chin and cheeks tickling me like well-used sandpaper. I chuckled and pulled my hands out from under my head to poke at him, and he pulled away, coming to sit upright beside me. His face turned and he smiled down at me, those mossy green eyes soft as he took in my body as though he was experiencing it for the first time again.

"I never get tired of our tree," he said.

"Me either."

"Do you think it will be here forever?" he asked. "Even after we're gone? Dead I mean."

"Morbid." I teased him.

He just smiled.

"Yes," I said, "I think it will be here long after we're dead. It will be a monument that we existed. Not me. Not you. *Us.*"

He sighed. "I like that."

I smiled and looked up at the canopy of leaves above us.

"But," he asked, "how is it proof that we were here? A tree isn't really proof of anything. Except that a sapling won its battle."

Thinking on this, I frowned as I stared up at the leaves and the beams of hazy late afternoon light peeking through. A quick thought, inspiration from the deepest part of me, overtook me and I sat up beside him. I retrieved the sketchpad I had tossed alongside the picnic bag and found the drawing I had done in the early morning hours by the creek. *My husband staring off at the horizon as the sun rose to greet the brand-new day.*

Deftly, I tore the piece of paper from the pad and rose to my feet. He watched me as I carefully folded it in half, then fourths, then eighths. Padding over on bare feet to the trunk of the tree, I found a knothole and slipped the rectangle of paper inside. Using my index finger, I pushed until it was so far into the dark crevice that it would never be discovered by a casual, searching eye. When I turned back to him, he was smiling oddly at me.

"I loved that sketch," he said.

"You love all of my sketches."

"They're all amazing, Ian," he said. "All of them."

I shrugged. "It wasn't my best, but it wasn't my worst. But now it will be proof—even if only you and I know it—that we were here."

He watched me for several moments.

"I suppose we can part with it for such a worthy cause," he said.

As I reached down to grab my shirt, Mike shook his head.

"Not yet," he said with a grin. "I don't want you to cover up yet. I'm enjoying the view."

"You always love the view, too." I teased.

"If that's a fault, I'll gladly own it."

"I wouldn't say as much," I said. "It's one of the things I love most about you, you know?"

"What?" He asked. "That I enjoy leering at you?"

"Even after all these years," I said with a nod. "Yes."

He laughed as his eyes were drawn to the horizon.

"Well," he said, "we've wasted the day, and—"

"I wouldn't call it *a waste.*"

He grinned. "—the sun will be going down soon. We have a promise to keep, you know."

"I don't like breaking promises," I said.

Mike stared at the horizon a moment longer as he grinned at the sun slowly traveling towards slumber. Then he rose to his feet, stared at the view my bare chest provided for a moment longer, then we returned our shirts to our torsos. We gathered up my sketchpad, our picnic bag, and hand-in-hand we walked away from our tree. Neither of us looked back, because looking back, giving the tree a final glance, was as if we were saying we expected to never see it again.

We both knew that to be false.

So why look back?

By the time we had made our way from the bank of the creek back into town, the sun was tucking itself away for the day and twilight was bearing down upon us. The fluorescent light of the convenience store—bars of neon white hanging from its eaves—shone down on us. The giant letters above the lights—"KC"—stared out at the rapidly growing main thoroughfare of our childhood town. Both of us couldn't help but smile up at those letters, standing there and basking in their white and red colors as we stood in the nearly empty parking lot.

Open All Day Long.

Unless We Have Better Plans.

That's what the sign in the front plate-glass window announced. It never failed to make me smile when I saw it.

Mike and I strolled through the newly installed automatic sliding glass door; our fingers still intertwined. The smell of industrial-strength cleaners and fruity slushy drinks permeated the air. Somewhere, hot dogs were being warmed. The flooring was fairly new—no longer yellowed old linoleum—middle of the road, dark wood laminate boards met our feet. The walls had been painted a light, yet cheerful blue and all of the light fixtures and displays had been brought into the twenty-first century.

"Luh-look who finally decided to show up." A voice reached our ears.

Mike and I turned, as one, and our eyes landed on the man behind the check-out counter.

"He huh-hasn't stopped tuh-talking about you two all day," Kevin beamed from his spot behind the register.

"At least he had something interesting to talk about," Mike said.

Kevin laughed and the two of us joined him at the checkout counter. Mike and I leaned against it, still holding hands, as Kevin regaled us with the day's events. Laughing, the three of us exchanged taunts and jabs, but mostly we talked about memories and what we'd missed since we had spent the day together in the woods and at the creek.

We hadn't gone to the convenience store, which our old friend co-owned, merely to relive old times or joke around with an old buddy. But we had time to indulge ourselves for a little while. After several minutes of talk, Kevin looked over our heads, and a smile broke out on his face.

"Huh-here they are," he said. "Did you guys finally find the puh-perfect candy bar?"

Mike and I turned in unison to find Carson—the other co-owner of the convenience store—walking toward us. He was smiling down at and talking to the small boy whose hand he was holding. When Carson—still sporting his *ZZ Top-esque* beard after so many years—heard Kevin's voice, his eyes were drawn from the boy and over to us. A grin bloomed on his face and he and the boy walked over to join us.

The five of us spent several minutes carrying on, discussing the day—the past—and everything in between, though the boy was growing visibly impatient with all of us.

When it became apparent that delaying things any longer would lead to whines and groans, I handed the picnic bag and sketchpad over to Kevin. He promised to keep them safe while we went on our next adventure.

"You guh-guys are a species of special concern," Kevin said as Mike and I each took one of the boy's hands in our own. "You'd rather be off in the woods looking at trees than indoors watching a movie."

Mike grinned at me.

"I hope that never changes," I said for the two of us.

Carson and Kevin waved us off as Mike and I made our way out of the store, the boy skipping merrily between us. As a unit, the three of us made our way back toward the creek, trailing through the inky-darkness of the town's streets.

"What did he mean?" The boy asked. "The species thing?"

Mike nodded at me in the darkness with a smile.

"Well," I said, "a *species of special concern* means that something—an animal, usually—is at risk of becoming threatened or extinct."

"Oh," the boy said. "What?"

"They don't make 'em like us anymore," Mike explained for me.

"Oh."

"Like the bats we're going to see," I said, explaining further. "We're in danger of being the last of a dying breed. Boys who would rather explore the woods than stay inside playing video games or watching T.V."

The boy rolled his eyes.

Point received, if not accepted.

As the three of us trailed through the dark woods, mine and Mike's memories navigating the underbrush and low-hanging limbs, the woods and its inhabitants whispered to us. Crickets played their violin legs and frogs belched their sonnets. Lightning bugs sent their morse code to potential mates.

When we finally reached the bank of the creek once more, the three of us stripped our pants off, leaving us in our swimsuits. The sultry summer night air licked at our flesh as I shimmied down into the creek and Mike held the boy's hands as he shimmied down to where I could catch him. The two of us stood in the creek, waist-high to me, nearly coming up to the boy's neck, as Mike navigated his way down to join us.

Once the three of us were in the water, we held hands and ventured out to the very middle. We stood in a line, holding hands, as we looked up at the full moon shining down on us. The boy shivered between us.

"Are you cold?" I asked.

"I'm okay," he said.

I took this for what it was. Even if he *was* cold, he wanted to see the bats.

"*Let's be very quiet,*" I whispered. "*Or we might scare them.*"

"*Okay,*" the boy said.

Mike just looked over and smiled, his teeth appearing nearly blue in the moonlight. For several minutes, the three of us stood there, holding hands, looking skyward in hopes of seeing our old friends, the bats. After a while, I began to worry that our journey to the creek at night was made in vain.

"*You know,*" I whispered to the boy, "*I used to come here at night for more than just the bats.*"

I wanted to give the boy something—*anything*—to make the trip out into the woods worthwhile. Just in case the bats decided not to show. I'd told him about them so many times that I didn't want him to leave disappointed.

"*Why did you come out here at night?*" He whispered his question back.

"*Sometimes,*" I said, "*I'd come out here to talk to God. Ask him questions.*"

That hung in the air around us as we all stared at the sky.

"*Did God ever answer?*" The boy whispered finally.

I smiled. "*He did.*"

"*How do you know?*" he asked.

I looked over at Mike and he was already looking over at me and smiling. I smiled back at him.

"*Sometimes God sends proof that he was listening,*" I said.

The boy accepted this for what it was, and Mike and I stared into each other's eyes, smiling as the boy looked to the sky. The water was warmer than I remembered it being many summers before, but it was still clear and clean, unsullied by the encroaching industry of a growing town.

Some things are too pure to be sullied.

"*Dad. Papa,*" the boy said. "*Look. The bats are here.*"

It took an effort, but Mike and I broke our gaze and turned our eyes to the sky. Small black bird-like streaks were swooping down from the trees to the water's surface, then swooping back up into the trees on the other side of the creek. Our bats had not forgotten their ballet.

The three of us stood there, Matthew—*our son*—clutching our hands gleefully as we watched the bats hunt for their dinner. Minutes ticked by as the bats swooped down and up, down and up, performing their nightly ritual while summer was still upon us.

"They'll be going home soon," I said. *"To Mexico."*

Matthew sighed.

"But won't they come back?" he asked, sounding worried as though he already missed them.

Again, Mike and I found each other's eyes. He smiled at me. Finally, I answered:

"Every chance they get," I said. *"As often as they can."*

About the Author

Chase Connor spends his days writing about the people who live (loudly and rent-free) in his head when he's not busy being enthusiastic about naps and Pad Thai. Chase started his writing career as a confused gay teen looking for an escape from reality. Ten years later, one of the books he wrote during those years, *Just A Dumb Surfer Dude: A Gay Coming-of-Age Tale*, was published independently. Now with The Lion Fish Press (and 20 books later), Chase has numerous projects in various stages of completion lined up for publishing. Chase is a multi-genre author, but always with a healthy dollop of gay.

Chase can be reached at
chaseconnor@chaseconnor.com
Or on Twitter @ChaseConnor7
He can also be found on Chase Connor Books
or on Goodreads

SIGN UP FOR THE CHASE CONNOR BOOKS NEWSLETTER AT CHASECONNOR.COM

He does his very best to respond to all DMs, emails, and Twitter comments from his reader friends and loves the interaction with them. Chase has several novellas/novels for sale in e-book, paperback, hardback, and audiobook formats wherever books are sold.